"Good

Logan whispered, knowing that Justine was out of earshot. He watched her go inside, turning out the light as she moved to her bed.

He continued to stand on the balcony for a long time, thinking not of the beauty of the night but of the beauty—and mystery—of the woman. When he'd reached for her hand, the sense of adventure that had possessed him all day had risen again, far more powerfully, inside him.

But the gesture had been an impulsive one, and Logan wasn't used to acting impulsively. He hadn't wanted to go any farther, to become a man recklessly plunging into a night in bed with Justine, the fabulous star. She was a woman whose mystery should be explored slowly... and he knew just how he would do that.

Dear Reader,

Spellbinders! That's what we're striving for. The editors at Silhouette are determined to capture your imagination and win your heart with every single book we published. Each month, six Special Editions are chosen with *you* in mind.

Our authors are our inspiration. Writers such as Nora Roberts, Tracy Sinclair, Kathleen Eagle, Carole Halston and Linda Howard—to name but a few—are masters at creating endearing characters and heartrending love stories. Their characters are everyday people—just like you and me—whose lives have been touched by love, whose dreams and desires suddenly come true!

So find a cozy, quiet place to read, and create your own special moment with a Silhouette Special Edition.

Sincerely,

The Editors
SILHOUETTE BOOKS

SE-RL-3A

ANNA JAMES
Their Song
Unending

Silhouette Special Edition

Published by Silhouette Books New York

America's Publisher of Contemporary Romance

SILHOUETTE BOOKS
300 East 42nd St., New York, N.Y. 10017

Copyright © 1987 by Madeline Porter and Shannon Harper

ISBN: 0-373-09371-3

First Silhouette Books printing March 1987

America's Publisher of Contemporary Romance

Printed in the U.S.A.

ANNA JAMES

has spent most of her time in either Atlanta, Georgia, or Los Angeles, California. She has written many different kinds of romances—from historicals to contemporaries, as well as numerous Gothics. When she's not traveling or writing, she enjoys tennis, the theater, long walks on the beach and her three incompatible cats.

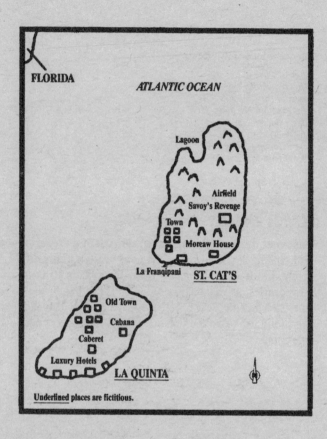

FLORIDA

ATLANTIC OCEAN

Lagoon

Airfield
Savoy's Revenge

Town
Moreaw House

La Franqipani

ST. CAT'S

Old Town

Cabana

Caberet

Luxury Hotels

LA QUINTA

Underlined places are fictitious.

Chapter One

"You really believe that Justine Hart is interested in La Quinta?" Logan Addison asked, looking up from the ledgers spread over his desk. He took off his horn-rimmed glasses and pushed them on top of his head before surveying his partner across the room.

Frank Norwood stood in the doorway and nodded. "You've got the figures there, pal. Wouldn't *you* be interested? The La Quinta Cabaret is going to turn that sleepy little island into one of the hot spots of the Caribbean."

"Probably," Logan answered as he folded up the charts and leaned back in his chair, unbuttoning the jacket of his three-piece suit. "It looks like a pretty solid investment; that is, as solid as anything can be outside of the continental U.S. The risks depend on the foibles of the tourist trade."

"Don't worry. The tourists are gonna flock to this place," his partner vowed, "especially with the night-club and casino."

"That's another problem," Logan said. "Does Justine know which of our clients are investing in La Quinta? Does she know they're calling it 'the cabaret that show biz built'?"

"Of course not," Frank responded as he dropped into a chair in his partner's office. "That's your rule—don't discuss one client's investments with another."

Logan nodded. "But this is a little different. It's going to be a very flashy operation, not just a good investment."

"Let me remind you old boy, that Justine Hart is a very flashy dame."

"But she's cautious, too. Granted, you know her better than I do. You're the one who gets all the personal conferences with her."

"Sure I do. I'm the front-office man," Frank said with a grin. "That's my style, as I reminded you when you left your father's stodgy firm to come in with me. Besides, as you may recall, that's how you wanted it, Logan. I deal with the clients, you deal with the books; that was the agreement. How are the books on this one, anyway—pretty good, huh?"

Logan didn't have to refer to the ledger; he had the figures in his head. "I agree that it's time to move some of Justine's funds out of stocks and bonds, and into real estate where there's a much better tax break, and with the shelter we'll get at La Quinta, it looks like a good investment."

"And she knows it. The lady doesn't just sing, she thinks, too, which you can't say about many of our other glitzy clients."

"That's the truth," Logan agreed as he considered the roster of Norwood and Addison clients.

"But I love 'em all," Frank declared, "especially the female rock stars. Hell, I even have a soft place in my heart for the old fogies."

Logan's responsive laughter crinkled the corners of his dark blue eyes. Then he returned his horn rimmed glasses to their solid perch on the bridge of his nose and looked down again at Justine Hart's prospectus.

Frank went on in the same vein. "Fortunately, we don't handle too many fogies. You left most of them behind at your family firm, thank the Lord. Do you ever regret it?"

"What?" Logan asked, looking up at his partner over the rim of his glasses.

"Leaving your Dad's place to join your old college buddy at the firm known irreverently as 'investors to the stars'?"

"Not a regret in the world," Logan answered.

After graduating from Princeton School of Business, Logan had joined the prestigious firm founded by his grandfather and presided over just as staidly and conservatively by his father. He'd been well suited there, or so he thought—until tempted by his college classmate. Frank's investment company was straining at the seams with a client roster that included many theatrical people and even a few rock stars. He needed the help of someone like Logan, an expert in the field, who carefully plotted out portfolios for clients and who, Frank admitted, was one of the smartest analysts in the field.

When Logan had argued that he wasn't the type to work with superstars, Frank had readily agreed. "Stay in the background," he'd suggested, "and I'll deal with the personalities." The balance had worked well. The partnership, now five years old, was very successful, having taken over a second floor in the most modern building on Wall Street. Nothing was somber about Norwood and Addison.

"Sometimes," Frank said, tilting his chair back on two legs, "I have a feeling that you're ready to break out further, shed the rep tie and the pin-striped suit and have a fling; that's why I think *you* should take Justine down to La Quinta."

"What?" Logan leaned across the desk and looked at his partner, whipping off his glasses.

"That's right. She just needs one little push and she'll be sold. I'm not trying to lead her into something because we need investors, Logan. You know as well as I do that we could get that place fully sold in no time—with our clients and people from the outside. But I think this is the one investment that would balance her portfolio. She needs it."

"And I'm elected to show it to her?"

"Has to be, old pal. Remember, I'm getting married in a few weeks, and I just don't think that Diane would be crazy about the idea of my running off to the islands with Justine Hart. In fact, she'd kill me."

Logan grinned in agreement.

"Besides," Frank went on, "Justine knows how I feel about La Quinta, and I don't want to push her any further. That's not the style to use with her on financial matters especially since her ex-husband Brady Hart bilked her for all she was worth. She's very suspicious, even of our firm, and we've handled her account for two years."

"That man must have been a smart operator," Logan murmured.

"A rat, to put it mildly. He recognized her talent and left his own band behind to make her a star. Brady was no fool; he knew that as Justine's manager he could pile up a fortune for himself."

"No wonder she's so suspicious."

"Don't you know the story?" Frank asked, surprised.

Logan shook his head.

"Well, he not only played around with her best friend but he stole her blind. Justine was a real innocent. She didn't know anything until after he died in that plane crash." Frank paused and looked over at his partner. "Obviously, you don't follow the tabloid scandals—and that's another reason you're such a good choice for the La Quinta trip."

"I'm supposed to allay her fears, is that it?"

"Yep." Frank smiled and ran one large freckled hand through his sandy hair. "That's the idea. She thinks of you as more cautious, more conservative— and maybe even a little brighter—than yours truly. The first two are perfectly true assessments, I'll admit. But not the last. Behind my ebullient facade—"

"Is an equally ebullient personality," Logan finished.

"True. But brains are hidden back there, too."

"Granted," Logan admitted, well aware that he never would have joined Frank's Wall Street firm if he'd had any doubts about that. Frank was smart, and he was honest, two traits Logan admired. He was also very knowledgeable in investment matters. They'd taken enough classes together at Princeton for Logan to find that out, and it had been proven again and again during the time they'd worked together.

"It's just that I hide my brains about as successfully as you hide your secret."

"Which is?" Logan's dark blue eyes narrowed quizzically.

"Your sense of adventure, pal. It's there. I got a hint of it in college, and I've been waiting all these years for you to break loose. It'll happen one day. Off will come the three-piece suit and then—watch out. It's very obvious on the squash court."

"That's competitiveness," Logan argued, "not adventurousness, my friend."

"They're closely related," Frank decided. "Anyway, maybe you can turn this trip to La Quinta into an adventure. Whatever happens, you're our behind-the-scenes man, and if you like the island and the setup there, she'll agree to the investment."

"And if I don't like it?"

"Then it's no go. Justine Hart is our biggest client. She's very important to the firm, and I sure don't want to screw up our relationship with her. So if you don't like the deal down there, say so. She trusts us, and I want her to keep on trusting us. You know how carefully she goes over every detail of her portfolio. One mistake and she'll walk out of here."

Logan nodded. "I'll give her the best advice I can." He got up and went over to the window of his office, a large expanse of glass from floor to ceiling that looked south to the tip of Manhattan and the twin towers of the World Trade Center, barely visible today through the shroud of fog. Frank had picked a good time to tempt him with the island sunshine. Logan turned to his partner. "So tell me more about the trip."

"She's just finishing up a week in Miami—*Justine at the Diplomat,*" he said impressively, for their client was one of the few women in the world known by her first name only. "So this is the perfect opportunity. She has a few days off, she's in the area, so to speak, *and* the lady likes to have a close look at her investments. It'll all work out.

"She'll meet you Monday morning at the Miami airport. I've chartered a plane to fly you to La Quinta for the day. You'll be back in time for a nine p.m. flight to New York."

"Only a day?"

"Wait a minute. Do I detect a little regret in your voice?"

Logan shrugged, but not quickly enough.

"Well, well. If I'd known..." Then Frank amended the thought. "No, Justine's not about to block out more than twelve hours."

"Well, since I've never spent more than ten minutes at a time with her, signing papers or explaining figures, twelve hours will be—"

"Long enough for you to become fascinated by the lady. I'm almost envious. In spite of Diane, I'll admit to a few fantasies about Justine myself. She's such a contrast—the flamboyant public personality and the serious, hard-nosed woman underneath. Quite a mystery, and one that would be intriguing to solve."

"Maybe it all stems from Brady Hart and what he put her through, hiding her true self."

Frank grinned. "Without the amateur psychoanalysis, we can say the lady is fascinating, sexy, mysterious—*and* you're looking forward to spending the day with her."

Logan turned away from the window and went back to his desk. "Yes, we can definitely say I'm looking forward to it. But I'm afraid there's no evidence that she feels the same."

Frank looked over at Logan and frowned slightly.

"What's the matter?" Logan queried.

"Well, now that I think about it, I've definitely noticed the way you look at Justine when she's in the office," Frank responded.

"But all *she* looks at, I'm afraid, is my balance sheet."

"For my ego's sake, I'd like to agree that you're right, but hidden somewhere in my memory is the real truth. Now that I'm on the threshold of becoming a married man, I'll have to admit it."

"And that is?" Logan was puzzled.

"It occurs to me that the look on her face was equally as interested as the look on yours."

Justine Hart crossed the lobby of her hotel followed by the manager, two bellboys, her publicist and her bandleader. The bill was taken care of in a matter of minutes, with quick scrutiny from Justine before she summarily dismissed the coterie, including her personal aides.

The time that had elapsed since Justine got out of the elevator was less than five minutes, but the lobby had already filled with curious guests, there to gawk at the woman who was so instantly identifiable. She never disappointed them, and today was no exception.

Her bright red hair hung with wild abandon to her shoulders and was just the color of her wide familiar mouth—seen so often in the closeups that ended her videos—and the frames of her huge glasses. She wore a fuchsia skirt, with a wildly flowered blouse and a bottle-green oversized jacket that covered her trim figure. To accommodate her "look," Justine wore spike-heeled sandals that gave height as well as presence to her less than impressive five-foot-four.

She took a manila folder from her secretary, jammed it into her already bulging tote bag and crossed the lobby toward the front door. Minions scattered ahead of her, opening doors and signaling for a cab.

Justine was always late, and this Monday morning was no exception. "I think you better step on it," she advised the cab driver.

"Late for your flight?" he asked over his shoulder as he weaved in and out of traffic to find a clear lane ahead.

"I'm supposed to be at the airport at nine o'clock."

The cabbie glanced at his watch. It was nine-thirty. "I'm afraid you've missed it," he informed Justine.

"It's a charter flight, and there's only one other passenger," she announced, a little worried as she added, "I'm sure he'll wait, but he's going to be upset. He's a very punctual type."

* * *

And in that spirit, with Justine as intimidated by Logan as he was by her, the two of them, so apparently different, reached the island of La Quinta, only an hour behind schedule.

The landscape, lush and tropical with splashes of orange frangipani, pink oleander and yellow hibiscus, was no more sensual than Justine, who was a touch of exotica among the more sedately coiffed and dressed women who toured the La Quinta facilities. For all Logan could tell, she didn't notice anyone else. She was intent on the business aspect of the trip as she walked beside him in her dangerously high heels, not missing a step, surprising him with the length of her stride. For such a little thing, he thought, she certainly had long legs.

They were accompanied on the tour by Señor Ortego, president of the management firm that handled La Quinta's publicity and public relations. Ortego, a handsome man dressed in a lightweight white suit, was facile with his words, smooth and charming but also quick with answers. He knew every inch of La Quinta, and he had no doubt about its future.

"We're located east of the highly trafficked part of the Caribbean," Ortego said with perfect diction, "and for some reason it took the developers a while to discover us. The Saints," he said with a grin, "were so appealing—St. Croix and St. Thomas and St. Martin—that this little Spanish-speaking island was hardly noticed."

"Well, it's noticed now," said Logan, looking out over the wide flat beach, as white and tempting as any of the beaches in the Caribbean. Along the water, three new hotels sprouted, clean and trim, built from the pinkish rock of the island. Behind them, nestled in the hibiscus trees, were two more hotels with separate bungalow units.

"On the opposite side of the island, there's another hotel in our little village. It's adobe and some people prefer it to the more modern structures. Of course, it's been renovated, and there's a pool and tennis courts. I'll take you there in my car," Ortego suggested.

As they drove along in the white convertible, Ortego described the island that was barely eight miles long and three miles wide. "A tiny paradise," he said, "complete with an airport for private planes and a natural harbor for yachts."

Justine smiled over at the handsome guide and remarked, "Then this is a playground for the rich and famous?" It was the first time she'd spoken to him directly. Her voice was low and throaty, and Logan noticed that Señor Ortego was entranced by it, entranced by *Justine*, just as Logan had been at the Miami airport that morning when she arrived—forty-five minutes late—a flash of color, wild hair and apologies.

He'd seen the hair first, red curls hanging to her shoulders. When they'd met in his offices, she'd always worn a bright scarf tied turban-style around her head. Because Logan had tried to seem as businesslike as possible, he hadn't noticed the red curls sticking out, or he *had* noticed but had tried not to imagine the rich color and texture of her hair.

Because he rarely watched TV and never went to rock concerts, Logan had never seen Justine except in the office setting. So the first view of her at the airport had been a surprise, the same surprise Señor Ortego seemed to be experiencing. Her voice had surprised Logan, too. She'd spoken rarely during their meetings and then in a soft near-whisper. Now, relaxed, she chatted happily with the two men, and her marvelously throaty voice intrigued them both.

As they drove along, Ortego answered Justine's question, remarking, "Cut-rate flights of tourists from New York, Atlanta or Houston don't come this way. We're thankful that there's no package deal to La Quinta. Often it's necessary, because of airline schedules, to spend the night in Guadeloupe before continuing on a private plane for our island. Of course," he added, "because you chartered a plane, you did not have such problem. Our visitors who fly their own planes have that advantage, too."

He pointed out the sights as they passed—the botanical gardens, the charming frame houses crowded along the narrow streets near a large natural harbor and the island women selling coral jewelry and spices from stands in the village. There they stopped to browse, explore the old hotel and sample a fruit punch made from one of the dozens of varieties on the island.

"Yes," said Señor Ortego contentedly. "Here in La Quinta we have everything—almost." He looked over at Logan with a twinkle in his eye. "We are missing only a casino-supper club, and that, very soon, we will also have. Would you like to see the building? It's almost completed; just the interior remains unfinished. In another month, we'll be ready to open."

"Señor Ortego," Logan said as they walked along the street toward the club, "have you always lived here on La Quinta?"

The Mediterranean features broke out in a grin as Ortego spoke. "I know why you ask me that question—because of my use of the pronoun 'we' and my great enthusiasm for La Quinta. Actually I have lived here only a little over a year. I was recruited right out of the University of Madrid to handle publicity for our island. You see, I say it again—*our* island—but I feel very much a native of La Quinta. It is a beautiful place, a warm and friendly place, and I am more at home here than in my native Spain. Ah, here we are," he exclaimed as they reached the end of the street.

The charm of the building was already apparent even though construction wasn't yet completed. It was a rambling frame building that looked like something from the 1930s with an added touch of Old World Spain.

"I feel like I've stepped into a Hemingway novel," Logan said, surprised. He'd seen only the flow sheets for the construction, never the actual plans.

"Yes," Ortego agreed. "That's the feeling we wanted to achieve. Inside, will be the casino and the stage, but even there we will maintain as much of the old world charm as possible. The food will also be Spanish with some of the flavor of the island in the shellfish recipes. We have hired one of the most famous chefs in Spain, direct from a three-star Barcelona restaurant. It's very unusual for a supper club to have such a high-class restaurant, but our patrons will be of the caliber to appreciate it. Of course, they will also appreciate the casino," he added with a grin.

"Not to mention the nightclub," Logan said.

"Ah, yes. We've already found great interest among the entertainers we've negotiated with. Who would not

want to perform in such an environment?'' he asked
rhetorically.

As they walked around the building, Logan watched
Justine's reaction to the Cabaret La Quinta. She listened carefully to Ortego's description. Then they
found an opening and climbed inside over piles of
construction materials. Even though much of the interior hadn't been completed, Justine seemed to be
able to visualize it. Logan noticed more than a vague
interest on her part. She liked the place, and possibly
not just from the standpoint of an investor. He wondered if, as Frank hoped, she could be persuaded to
perform here.

Ortego, if he had that same thought, didn't express
it; he was much too circumspect. But he didn't fail to
remind Justine that all the sound and lighting equipment was being ordered from the United States; in
fact, from a company in Los Angeles that she knew to
be one of the best.

Because there was a strong light through the un-
paned windows and partially open roof, Justine didn't
remove her huge red sunglasses. With them in place,
Logan couldn't see her eyes to interpret her thoughts,
but he doubted if he could have known what she was
thinking even if the glasses had been removed. He
could only wonder.

In the office, on those brief occasions when he'd
met with her, Logan had found her surprisingly
knowledgeable. It hadn't been necessary to explain
anything more than once. Now he was beginning to
wonder what else there was to Justine Hart besides her
obvious talent—which he'd recently discovered for

himself after purchasing a few of her albums—and her sharp mind.

He had a terrible urge to find out what kind of woman she was, but while she'd been polite, even friendly, nothing about her gave Logan the feeling that he'd ever get past the flamboyant facade. He doubted, in fact, if she'd ever even take off her glasses in his presence. As the day wore on he began to think of them as a symbol of the distance separating him and Justine. He knew what color her eyes were from photographs on her album covers, but he wanted to see for himself.

"In our newest hotel, just being completed, we already have eighty percent of the rooms reserved," Ortego was telling them. "I can foresee that cabaret seats could be very hard to come by once the island becomes even more popular. Already, we've had inquiries: 'Should I book the club before the hotel?' they ask." He laughed. "Frankly, I'm not sure how to answer that. It would be unfortunate to come to La Quinta and find yourself with a room but no show. However, it would be worse to get here and have a table at the cabaret but no room!" he said, laughing.

"The audience here will be fairly small," Justine commented as she looked around the room from the stage.

"Just as we planned. We want to limit attendance at the shows and in the casino to a select patronage. This isn't going to be Atlantic City. Here, we will have a little class," he said with a grin.

"But great wealth along with all that class," Logan suggested.

"Ah, yes," Ortego agreed. "It is obvious that the casino will make huge profits from our clientele." Taking a white handkerchief from his pocket, Ortego wiped his forehead and then replaced his Panama hat. The heat was beginning to wilt his white linen suit.

Logan, too, was feeling slightly rumpled as they stepped back into the bright sunshine. He'd unbuttoned the jacket of his cream-colored suit and had even considered loosening his tie. Justine, however, looked as bright and fresh as when they'd started out, hurrying along beside the men in her high-heeled sandals.

Climbing back into the convertible, Ortego headed toward the hotel district of the island. "I thought you might enjoy a cool drink before returning to Miami," he suggested.

"That sounds like a good idea," Logan said, watching for Justine's reaction.

"Yes, I'd like a drink, something tall and icy, an island specialty," Justine answered.

"In that case, I will take you to the perfect place, not a hotel after all but a little cabana right on the beach. It is more secluded there because it's a rather long walk from the road. You don't mind?" he asked, confident of the answer.

Everything went smoothly as long as Ortego remained at the cabana with them, discussing the day's events and answering questions. When he left for another appointment, Logan experienced a moment of unaccustomed discomfort. He'd never had any such feelings during meetings with Justine. Even on the flight from Miami, he'd been friendly if not totally relaxed. But this setting was meant for something other than business meetings.

The little cabana was rustic and romantic with glass and wicker tables, comfortable cushioned armchairs and very tall rum and fruit drinks. Overhead fans caught the breeze from the sea and stirred it around lazily. It wasn't a place to discuss business; it was a place for intimacy.

Yet Logan couldn't picture himself here with any other woman. No one else quite fit in the cabana. "Your choice of women is much too tweedy," was Frank's assessment of everyone Logan had introduced him to. "Pale and overly sophisticated," he'd added. "But I do remember a couple of gals you were interested in at school who were my idea of the real thing."

"That was a long time ago," Logan had countered. "I'm a lot more sensible now."

"Well, maybe that's the word," Frank had said with a laugh, "but if you're so sensible, I wonder why you never have found the right one out of all those refined blond types?"

Logan hadn't been able to answer that.

"Well, what do you think?" Justine asked, taking off her sunglasses and bringing him back to the present with a jolt. At first he interpreted that as a sign that the business part of their day was over and their personal relationship could begin. Then he realized that it was dark in the cabana, and she'd simply removed the glasses so she could *see*. Justine was still all business.

Equally businesslike, Logan responded, "I can't refute anything that Ortego says. We can go over the prospectus again, but all his figures check out. The problem might be attracting the kind of top entertainment that's needed here."

"But Señor Ortego said—"

"I know," Logan answered. "There's 'great interest' among the entertainers they've contacted. Naturally. He would hardly say otherwise. But I'd like to see a few contracts before I'm thoroughly convinced."

Justine brushed that remark aside. "I can't imagine not wanting to perform here. The equipment is going to be the very best. The stage has plenty of depth without losing intimacy. And the rest—it's a paradise."

Logan found himself listening to her voice instead of her words, and he had to stop for a moment to get what she'd actually *said* into his mind. Then he answered carefully. "Paradises can be deceiving."

"Are you telling me not to invest here?"

Her eyes were brown, a deep, deep color that couldn't begin to be captured in the photographs. He wanted to ask her why she *ever* wore dark glasses; instead he answered her question. "No, I'm not telling you that at all. Obviously, your investing here would be good for us—for Norwood and Addison—but I think you should be very careful. It's easy to be seduced by all this," he said. Something in those words tripped him, made him hesitate before getting back on track, for he was feeling seduced by La Quinta himself. "Wait until we return to New York and review everything once more, very carefully; wait until we see a couple of contracts. Then make your decision.''

She looked at him speculatively. "Frank was right to send you. He would have given me the hard sell, and I would have backed away. Instead you're subtly dangling the cabaret in front of me, and I'm intrigued.''

Logan had begun to feel comfortable in the little cabana beside this unusual woman who was not his type at all, who mystified him and who, he admitted, had been a vague fantasy of his for a long time. Why else would he have bought those albums? Why else would he have agreed to come on this trip? He could have refused; they could have very well sent another partner.

But he hadn't refused. It would have been a good day's work for Norwood and Addison if Justine decided to invest in La Quinta. Yet he hadn't come for that but to see her brown eyes flashing in the pale skin, her wild red hair and her…mystery. Dress and makeup and just plain style had turned her into Justine. She wasn't a beautiful woman. She was a woman who'd made the most of what she had and then settled back to let people figure out the rest. That was the mystery.

"You're a smart lady who knows her own mind," Logan said. "I'll give you all the guidance I can in this matter, but ultimately you'll make the decision yourself. I think it'll be the right one.''

That satisfied Justine, who was trying hard not to be captivated by the man sitting opposite her. This was a business associate, and she had long ago sworn never to mix business with her personal life. But she was intrigued by Logan Addison, especially now, in the intimate little cabana, where their table was secluded in a corner away from the few customers who had straggled in from the beach for a cool drink.

For the first time since she'd met him almost two years before, Justine was seeing Logan relax. He'd taken off his jacket, which she never would have expected—even in the Caribbean heat. His beige shirt was damp, clinging to his chest and upper arms and revealing a musculature that Justine had known was there beneath the three-piece suit. He was a squash player; she'd found that out inadvertently, when he'd rescheduled an afternoon appointment around his workout at the gym. Well, it showed.

She looked away and mentally clothed him in the jacket again and mentally straightened the tie that he had finally decided to pull loose.

"Would you like another drink?" Logan asked. He'd taken off his glasses, too, and pushed them on top of his head, burying them in his thick dark hair. She tried to ignore the fine texture of his hair and then made the mistake of looking into his eyes. They were just the color of the sky at midnight when the stars gave enough illumination to turn it a bright blue-black.

"No," she answered quickly, "thank you, but we should really be thinking about getting back to the airport. We don't want to keep the pilot waiting—again," she added with a wry smile.

"No, that would never do," Logan answered, returning her smile.

The plane was on the runway, engines revving. They stood for a moment at the grassy edge of the tarmac and looked around. "In a way, I hate to leave," Justine said. "You're right, it is seductive."

"You'll be back," Logan said as he took her arm and led her toward the plane, not sure why he thought she'd be back but somehow certain she would—and that he would, too.

Justine felt at home in the private plane; she was a star and rarely flew on commercial flights. What was different this time was the company she was keeping—one of New York's top investment counselors, a man who was cut from an entirely different pattern than her own. His background was solid, probably stretching back for generations. It was something that couldn't be manufactured. On the other hand, everything about Justine Hart was manufactured, starting with her name. She'd grown up as Clara Johnson. It had never suited her, and she'd changed it the day that Brady Hart took her away from her small Georgia hometown to begin a new life in which she had it all.

At least she had it for a while, until she found out the man she'd entrusted with her career, and her life, had betrayed her. Suddenly Justine felt a rush of gratitude for Logan Addison. She'd searched carefully and made a wise choice in Norwood and Addison, but she'd been lucky, too, in finding not only talent and skill in her financial advisors but honesty.

In her seat opposite him across the narrow aisle, Justine watched as Logan shuffled through his La Quinta papers, and she thought about what made him so interesting. It certainly wasn't his businesslike manner or even his hidden muscles. He was honest, sincere. He had the kind of manners and charm that she'd never come in contact with before. She supposed it was called class, although from her childhood in Georgia to her sudden fame as a rock star, she'd never encountered it. Yet something told her she'd been searching for it all her life.

Justine smiled over at Logan, and when he looked up, she said quietly, "Thanks for all the trouble you've taken with me today."

"It's my job," Logan replied. "After all, you're our number-one client."

As soon as the words were out, he realized how cold they sounded. He'd missed the opportunity that he'd been waiting for all day, the chance to say something that would put their relationship on a more personal level. But before he could correct the mistake, a loud rumbling shook the plane. It began to career and lose altitude, quivering violently in the process, and Logan instinctively reached across the aisle for Justine's hand.

Chapter Two

Justine clutched the strong hand that held hers. Her fingernails dug into Logan's skin as if releasing him or losing hold would fling her alone into an unending void. Then the plane plunged, suddenly, violently. It fell hundreds of feet in a few seconds, dropping with such force that everything in the cabin—her bag, Logan's briefcase, the newspapers and magazines—was flung to the ceiling, and Justine's body strained against the seat belt that held fast.

The downward plunge suddenly ended as the plane leveled and began to climb. For a moment Justine's grip on Logan's hand eased. Then the quivering began again with such force that she was sure the plane would be torn apart. Her eyes were closed tightly, and at first she didn't realize what was happening when Logan placed his other hand on top of hers and gently but firmly began to peel her fingers away from his. Her eyes shot open.

"It's all right, Justine, you're going to be all right. Just hold on to the armrest," he said, moving her hand away.

"What—" Her voice was hoarse. The word didn't even escape her lips but caught somewhere in her throat.

"I'm going up front now," he said with such evenness of voice, such calmness, that Justine looked across the aisle to make sure it was Logan speaking. "Don't worry."

With that, he unbuckled his seat belt and stood up, reaching for the overhead rack as he made his way toward the front of the plane. Just as he took the last few steps, the violent shaking threw him forward into the hatch and flung it open as he fell inside. He regained his balance and closed the door behind him, and Justine was alone in the cabin of the plane.

The glimmer of hope that they'd survive this terrible, inexplicable thing that was happening was gone with Logan, gone with the loud thumping that shook the plane, gone with the speed at which it was being flung through the air. She could only curse him under her breath for leaving her when certainly there was nothing he could do in the cockpit. He wasn't a pilot, for God's sake, she thought furiously to herself; he was a financial advisor. What in the world could he do but make things worse?

Somehow, cursing Logan helped to transfer her fright into anger so that when the engines cut off suddenly and they began to glide, Justine felt a sort of peace come over her. She looked out of the window, and even in the gathering twilight, she could make out the line of the horizon against the sky. But it was getting closer and closer. They were going to crash!

She tried to close her eyes, but something made her keep them open, wide and frightened, to watch as the dark line of the horizon became clear and the outline of trees rushed by at eye level, flashing like pages flipped in a child's book, faster and faster, just beyond the window of the plane.

Justine felt the jolt when they hit the ground, bounced up and then hit again with such a force that her head was whipped forward. But she didn't even notice the pain as her forehead banged against the seat in front. She could only envision the coming crash, the explosion and the flames as the plane and the three people in it became a red ball of fire in the jungle of some Caribbean island.

The image was so vivid that Justine could almost hear the explosion in her head, feel the heat and see the consuming flames. With her eyes tightly shut, grasping the armrests and forcing herself back against the seat, she prepared for her end.

A moment—an eternity—passed and suddenly everything was still. For a long time she remained motionless, as if waiting for the rest, the Armageddon that was sure to follow. Nothing followed but silence and then a voice. Logan's voice.

"Justine, Justine," he called from what seemed like a million miles away.

Slowly she opened her eyes. There was no smoke, no flames. There was only the cabin, just as before, except that it looked like a hurricane had come through, upsetting everything that wasn't bolted down. Beyond the clutter, standing at the door of the cockpit, was Logan.

He looked the same—cream-colored suit, carefully knotted tie, vest. Even his glasses were still in place, and for some reason that made Justine smile and then, suddenly, begin to laugh.

It was a laugh of relief more than hysteria. Logan realized that as he made his way down the aisle to her. Nevertheless, he grabbed hold of her arms and gave her a little shake. "Justine," he said almost sternly, "it's over."

"What . . . happened?" she asked, looking up into his dark blue eyes and wondering how he could possibly be so calm. He showed no fear, not even any real concern.

From the front of the plane, Steve, the pilot, appeared. He looked pale under his coffee-colored skin, his eyes dilated and wild, but he managed to grin. "I wish I *knew* what happened," he said, shaking his head. "I've never seen an engine malfunction like that in all the years I've been flying." He collapsed in the seat across from Justine. Logan remained standing beside her.

"I think an electrical malfunction must have triggered the whole thing," Logan observed.

Steve nodded in agreement. "That we got through at all is a miracle. Someone's been living right!"

"It was probably Justine's aura," Logan said as his eyes caught hers and held until she found herself looking away.

"That and your help," Steve responded. "Don't know what I'd have done if you hadn't found this island on the map. I sure couldn't fly and read the aerials at the same time," he told Justine. "I was flying blind." He looked up at Logan with admiration. "You had experience as an aviator?"

"I've done a little flying," Logan admitted.

"Well, you read maps like a charm."

"Funny thing is," Logan said, leaning over Justine to look out the window, "there was no runway marked, and yet we're on a runway."

"And a pretty good one at that, built for twin engine planes even larger than this one. What's the name of this place?"

Logan consulted the maps he'd brought from the cockpit. "St. Catherine's. Looks like mostly hilly terrain. This is probably the only level ground on the island. But if there's a runway, there's bound to be a town—and a radio."

"What about the plane's radio?" Justine asked, finally beginning to come back to life, realizing that they were grounded on an island she'd never heard of—and she was supposed to be in New York in the morning.

"It was the first thing to go," Steve said, standing up and pushing his cap back into his black curly hair. "I guess we better see what's out there," he suggested to Logan.

"Wait here," Logan said to Justine as he followed Steve to the back hatch. They opened it and lowered the ramp while Justine remained, obediently, in her seat, her belt still secure around her. In spite of everything that had happened and her lingering fright, she realized with a shock that she was thinking not about the plane's near miss, but about Logan Addison.

He didn't seem like the same person. Since the moment he'd reached for her hand, something had been

added to the traits she'd admired and which had separated him from the hangers-on who'd once been a
part of her life. They were unexpected additions—authority, strength and even a sense of adventure. She'd
seen a flash in his eyes when she'd looked at him and
expected to find fear there. What she'd found was excitement.

Justine breathed an audible sigh and leaned back
against the seat, exhausted from what she'd been
through. Her head was beginning to throb, too. She
remembered hitting her forehead on the seat. Reaching up, she felt that a bump had begun to form just
above her eyebrow. Well, makeup would hide it, she
told herself, relieved that she was alive.

Loud voices called out in the night, and Justine
leaned forward and looked out the window as three
men, dressed in khaki shirts and wearing pith hel-
mets, drove onto the runway in a Jeep.

Her fear quickly returned, and Justine began to
tremble. Just after they'd managed, by some miracle,
to find a place to land the plane, they were being at-
tacked! She forced herself to look out the window
again only to see that the men who approached weren't
armed.

Unbuckling the seat belt, Justine got up and went to
the back of the plane, where she could see and hear
but still remain out of sight behind Logan and the
pilot.

The shouting continued, and Justine realized it
wasn't in English or Spanish. Then she heard Steve
murmur, "Oh, great. We're on a French-speaking
island."

Justine was able to make out the words *"Allez-vous-en"* as one of the men waved his hand demandingly, obviously urging them to get back on the plane and leave.

"It's all right," Logan assured Steve. Climbing down the stairs, he called out a greeting and began to speak in rapid French, another surprise from this man who was full of surprises.

One of the three men, tall and dark skinned, stepped forward. Logan crossed to meet him, and Steve followed a little way behind.

Logan continued to speak in French, and Justine was able to catch a few words. She knew the language slightly from trips she'd made abroad, and she could tell that Logan's accent was perfect, his voice very confident. But the leader still didn't look friendly, nor did the other two men who stood menacingly beside him.

As Logan spoke, pointing to the plane and the pilot and then gesturing in what Justine assumed was an explanation of their near crash, the men didn't change expression, and Justine could only be glad that they weren't carrying guns.

The response to Logan's discourse came in a few clipped sentences causing Logan to turn back to Steve, shaking his head. "He wants us to *move* the plane." Justine could see Logan struggling to remain patient as once more he described what had happened.

The answer was, again, fast and clipped, and when the man stopped speaking, his two friends climbed into the Jeep and drove it toward the plane.

"What's happening?" Steve asked.

Logan shrugged.

"Do they have a radio?" was Steve's next question.

"Yep," Logan told him. "But it's on the owner's plane, and he's in the States."

"Damn," Steve muttered.

"Looks like our only choice is to head for civilization."

"What about the plane?" Steve said. "It belongs to my charter company. They'll kill me if—"

Logan interrupted. "They'll most likely promote you, Steve, when they find out you managed to save their plane from crashing."

"But what about these guys . . . ?" Steve motioned toward the two men in the Jeep, who'd hooked a hitch up to the plane.

"I suggest we leave them to their objectives."

"Wait a *minute*," Steve protested, "they're dragging off my plane!"

Logan put a restraining hand on the pilot's arm. "I don't think we're in a position to argue." He smiled, and Justine couldn't help thinking what a relaxed smile it was. "In fact, I've already argued in my best French, and gotten nowhere. Their boss, whoever he is, owns this place."

"But—" Steve began, pushing his cap farther back on his head.

"And we don't want your plane, your company's plane," Logan amended, "sitting out there in the middle of the airfield when this guy comes home and tries to land *his* plane."

"What'll we do?" Steve asked.

"They tell me there's a town two miles west of here. I think we better head for it. Someone's bound to have a radio."

"Walk?" Justine had finally ventured down the stairs to stand beside the pilot and Logan. "We can't walk," she cried. Beyond them was nothing but jungle, heavy ferns and giant trees festooned with vines. Somewhere in the mass of deep green an unidentifiable animal called out. Night would be upon them soon, the deep thick impenetrable night of the tropics.

"They don't seem inclined to offer us a ride," Logan said with an ingratiating smile. "Believe me, I've done what I can to persuade them, and I feel certain that any more arguing will just cause us more trouble." With that Logan headed out across the runway. Steve shrugged and fell in behind him. Justine stood still for no more than a few seconds before taking a deep breath and following.

At the edge of the runway there was a road, wide enough for the Jeep to pass through but rutted and muddy from recent tropical rains. It led up a steep hill. Logan's map had been right about the mountainous terrain.

Looking to the left as they reached the foot of the hill, Steve let out a low whistle and Justine's gaze followed his. There in the jungle was a mansion, a brick two-story house with a wide veranda set in a clearing of impeccable lawns, formal gardens and marble statuary.

"Belongs to the owner of the airstrip," Logan informed them as he walked on. Steve and Justine, still gaping at the edifice, tried to keep up with him. Justine's high heels that had been no problem on La Quinta, were going to be a big problem here. She was determined to manage.

The determination faltered very quickly, however, as the road narrowed and the ruts deepened. She stumbled on, looking daggers into Logan's back, but his long, effortless stride didn't slacken. And as he walked he carried on a running commentary about the varieties of foliage, the jungle birds asleep on branches high above them and the animal sounds coming from the depths of the jungle. Justine remained silent, although she was tempted to remind him that some of those marvelous night noises might be emanating from less than friendly animals.

As Justine quickened her pace to keep up with Steve and Logan, the ruts that at first had exasperated her finally defeated her completely. "Logan," she called out, "wait a minute, my—" She'd caught her heel in a rut where it stayed, firmly imbedded in the hardened mud, while she went on walking, one shoe off and one shoe on.

"Shall I carry you?" he asked with a wry smile as he retraced his steps and came to a halt beside her.

"No," Justine said defiantly, pulling off her other shoe.

While Logan and Steve stopped to see what would happen next, Justine, with a triumphant look first at one of them and then at the other, tossed the shoe as far as she could into the night.

"Wow," Steve said admiringly as he watched it sail off. "Some arm."

"Now what?" Logan asked.

"I walked barefoot a lot as a child in the red mud of Georgia," Justine said. "I can do it here."

"Might as well take off your stockings, too," Logan suggested as he politely looked away.

"I never wear stockings," came the response, and Justine wondered if her words had brought a blush to Logan's face. But since he was turned away, she'd never know.

They trudged on, following the road until they reached a clearing, where it widened and joined another path from the left. "This is the halfway mark," Logan told them.

"We *must* have walked more than a mile—"

He shook his head. "Jungle miles seem longer, especially in this terrain," he said, and Justine wondered how he knew that, sitting in his office in Wall Street. But she'd also wondered how the conservative, staid Logan Addison had learned to fly a plane. He was probably wondering about her, too. Not too many people knew about her Georgia dirt farm upbringing, but something, perhaps plain defiance, had made her tell him about going barefoot as a child. Forging on, Justine wondered at how much they had learned about each other in the aftermath of such a close call.

At last civilization came into view, or at least one house at the side of the road and in the distance, flickering lights. They walked beside a cultivated field on the slope of a hill, where a few goats stood sleeping, hardly disturbed by the strangers who passed nearby. Following alongside the field, they came up to the house. It was painted a faded turquoise with white shutters and surrounded by a stone wall. As they

passed through the gate and walked into the courtyard, a light came on above the door.

"Qu'est-ce que c'est?" a voice called out. The door
opened and a gray-bearded man stepped onto the
porch. Justine saw the smile on his ebony face and felt
relief. At least he was friendly, although French
speaking.

Logan began to explain their predicament. The
older man listened politely, and when Logan stepped
back, he answered in English that was halting and
heavily accented but quite understandable.

"Welcome, lady and gentlemen." One arm swept
forward with a flourish. "Welcome to my home. I am
Emil Moreau."

Logan introduced himself, Justine and Steve. The
old man smiled at each in turn and then said, "I think
some refreshment for you?"

Justine nodded and sank into the chair he offered.
Logan stood beside her. "Something to drink would
be appreciated," he said.

"Angelique—" their host called out.

A pretty young woman with skin the color of *café
au lait* appeared at the door. She wore a white blouse
and a brightly flowered skirt, and her dark hair hung
loose to her shoulders. She smiled shyly at the
strangers.

"This is my daughter," the bearded man informed
them.

Steve, who'd just sat down in one of the twig-
constructed chairs on the porch, got up quickly and
bowed from the waist. *"Bonjour,"* he said.

The girl answered in a pretty, rich voice, *"Bon-
soir."*

"It's nighttime, Steve—*soir*, not *jour*," Logan offered.

"My daughter also speaks some English," her father declared. "Bring some mango and pineapple juice for our guests. And for the lady," he added with a glance at Justine's bare and muddy feet, "a pair of sandals." He turned to Logan. "Here I have many pairs of sandals which are sold in the village and also sent to other islands. Very good quality," he added, "and the lady, I think, is in need of a pair."

Logan laughed and explained their trek from the airfield along the difficult road.

"You were very lucky to have found St. Catherine's. Not all of the islands have an airstrip. It is a private field, belonging to Monsieur Graham. He has lived here for many years. You saw his fine home? My daughter works for him," he said proudly.

Angelique reappeared, carrying a tray with glasses and two pitchers.

"Here, let me help you." Steve took the tray, put it on a table and poured tall glasses of juice for the four of them.

"And for you?" Steve asked the young girl, whose response was to shake her head and step back under the eaves where she stood quietly, barely visible in the shadows.

"The sandals, Angelique," her father reminded the shy girl.

She reached just inside the doorway and brought out several pairs, which she placed beside Justine's chair before stepping quickly away.

The first pair fit perfectly, but before Justine could reach for her purse, Logan had taken out his wallet to pay for them.

"For our new friends, I make a good price," Monsieur Moreau said with a grin. "Ten American dollars. That is a bargain, is it not?" Shaking his head in agreement and with a slight smile, Logan paid for the shoes. "Now," the older man said, satisfied, "how else may I help?"

"Well, if you have a radio—"

"Yes," Angelique said without stepping from the shadows. "I have a radio."

"That is not what our guests mean, Angelique," the old man told his daughter. "You wish a radio to send messages?"

"Yes," Steve answered, "a ham radio—short-wave. Do you know where we can find one?"

"There is such a radio on St. Cat's—in the shop of Martin Lamont."

"Thank goodness," Justine said. Tired and bruised, she wanted to get off this island and back to New York. "We can call for help and the charter company will send someone."

"Not tonight," Steve cautioned. "We got lucky, thanks to my copilot here. But my company's not going to chance sending another plane to an uncharted field at night."

"No, we'll have to wait until morning," Logan agreed.

"In any case," Monsieur Moreau told them, "you will have to wait until morning to send the message. It is now after nine o'clock. Martin has closed his shop and gone down the hill to the café." He smiled and shook his head, "And by this time, he is quite drunk."

"Great," Justine said, becoming even more irritated.

"We'll get to the radio first thing in the morning," Steve assured her.

"And we will all hope that the radio is working," Monsieur Moreau added with a grin that brought another groan from Justine. "Often it is not."

Steve, who'd managed to persuade Angelique to sit down in a twig chair beside him, seemed totally uninterested in whether the radio worked or not.

"You will need to stay the night in St. Cat's," Monsieur Moreau said. "For my extra bedroom, I make you a good price."

"Is there a hotel in the town?" Logan asked, knowing that Justine wasn't about to spend the night in the jungle.

"Yes, there is, a very fine one," Monsieur Moreau admitted.

"Well," Steve drawled, no more interested in the town than the radio, especially when there was a room right here—in Angelique's house. "I'll volunteer to stay here for the night." His voice had a trace of martyrdom in it, which didn't fool Justine or Logan—and probably didn't fool anyone else on the porch, either.

"We would welcome you," Monsieur Moreau said. His daughter ducked her head and blushed.

Justine was only relieved that she wouldn't have to stay in the little house, happy to take a chance finding a room in the hotel, even if it meant more walking. Logan, who'd noticed her restlessness, asked a few more questions about the hotel, seemed satisfied that they'd find comfortable accommodations there and bade their host goodbye. Then he headed down the road with Justine, wearing her comfortable sandals, beside him.

As they neared the town, the road was smoother and wider, bordered by a low wall reminiscent, Logan told Justine, of the French countryside. She couldn't help countering with the remark that she, too, had traveled in France.

"Of course," Logan replied. "I'm sure your music has taken you all over the world." After a moment of silence he added, "But you probably had no idea you'd ever visit St. Catherine's island."

Not amused, Justine stubbornly didn't answer, and Logan continued his comments on the beauty of their surroundings. Closer to town they passed frame homes painted bright colors, washed clean by recent rains and bubbling with musical voices from within. On some of the porches, older members of the family sat quietly rocking and smoking, the pipes billowing white wisps into the black night.

"Yes," Logan said, almost to himself, now that Justine was quietly and not very pleasantly silent at his side, "it's a beautiful place."

"I think you're really enjoying all this," she said finally. "We're stranded on an island no one ever heard of, heading toward a town with a hotel that may or may not have rooms, and if it does, may or may not be liveable, in search of a radio owned by an alcoholic!"

Logan started to laugh and finally, unable to keep a straight face any longer, she joined in.

"Think of it as an exciting adventure—lost in the jungles of the Caribbean. We're cut off from the rest of the world and no one knows where we are. Of course, you're stranded with your financial advisor, which isn't so romantic. But *I'm* with the famous Justine Hart. Not bad," he said with a grin.

But Justine was still a few words behind. "Stranded," she repeated. "They're probably wondering what in the world happened to us! I imagine Frank is very worried. Maybe somebody's already out searching..."

Logan shook his head. "Frank's out on the town with Diane, and he hasn't given us a thought. Even if I don't turn up at work in the morning, he'll probably assume I'm resting from the trip. The same for the people on your staff. No one's going to begin worrying until tomorrow night at least, and by then we'll be in touch with them. So let's enjoy the rest of the evening."

"I plan to—with a bath, dinner in my room if that's possible and a good night's sleep."

Those words ended Logan's enthusiasm. He knew that his enjoyment of the whole episode was due to the fact he was sharing it with Justine. Unfortunately, she wasn't at all interested in her partner in the experience. Once or twice, at La Quinta and then on the plane, he'd thought, maybe hoped, there was a glimmer in her eyes that could have been interpreted as curiosity or interest. But since their trek through the hills began, the only look he'd seen there, after the fear disappeared, was anxiety and irritation. She wanted to be in New York, not on St. Catherine's. She was interested in comfort, not romance.

* * *

The hotel was tucked into the side of a hill with an entrance on a courtyard and a view of the ocean, with its crescent beach and small fleet of fishing boats. La Frangipani Inn seemed to have risen out of the dream that was St. Catherine's, for the town, too, was a colorful gem in a dark green setting of lush tropics.

"I can't believe it," Justine said, unable to restrain her appreciation. "Why do you suppose this little island hasn't been *discovered*?"

"Probably because the peripatetic 'Monsieur Graham' owns the airfield on the only level ground. You remember all the hills," Logan said, knowing full well that Justine hadn't forgotten. "But an occasional tourist must reach St. Cat's somehow," he added as they walked into the front door of the inn, "or this place wouldn't be here."

At the desk they found out that, indeed, tourists came to St. Cat's by ferryboat from other islands. Many of them French, they came in small numbers but because of the difficulty in gaining access to the island, they often stayed on and on, some for the whole season or even the whole year. Out of the ten available rooms, there were two vacancies, adjoining rooms with an ocean view.

"Ask if there's a restaurant," Justine urged Logan.

The answer was yes, there was a restaurant, serving island dishes including a delicious conch soup. And, yes, came the answer to Justine's next question, room service was available.

As they climbed the curving stairway to the second floor, Logan couldn't help but recall her question about room service. Obviously she had every intention of doing just as she'd told him earlier—having a bath, dinner in her room and a good night's sleep. Well, Logan thought, so much for his fantasy about being alone with Justine Hart in an island paradise.

They let themselves into their separate rooms with shared glances, followed by uneasy smiles. Justine closed the door behind her and looked around her room. It was furnished with rough copies of a French country armoire, table, ladder-back chair and four-poster bed, all obviously made from the wood of island trees and carefully painted in rich tones of red and green and yellow. Under other circumstances, Justine told herself, she would have been charmed by the island and the inn. Now she was only annoyed that she was here rather than in New York, where she was expected. No, that wasn't the whole truth, she admitted, sinking onto the bed.

She'd been thinking of the Logan Addison she'd discovered in the past few hours and somehow been afraid of the vision that those thoughts had conjured up. To all the adjectives she'd used to describe him to herself—honest, intelligent, sophisticated—had been added his commanding way of taking charge, a trait that frightened her in its appeal. She had a feeling that because she was becoming so susceptible to the man who'd gotten them out of a potentially bad situation and into a comfortable inn for the night, it would be best to avoid him.

That's why she'd decided to have dinner in her room, not because she didn't want to dine with him in the restaurant overlooking the Caribbean, tasting the apparently famous conch soup and spicy entrées, sipping rum punch or whatever exotic drink was offered. She wanted that very much, which was why she refused it. Justine had complete control over her life now, and she was afraid of losing it. Somehow, she was a little afraid of Logan Addison.

She peeled off her jacket, skirt and blouse, stepped out of the flimsy chemise, which was all she wore under her clothes, and walked naked across the room to the bath. It was small but adequate, with an old-fashioned footed tub. She turned on the taps and let the water run almost to the top. Then Justine sank down into the water and soaked away the day's dirt and pain, putting a cool washcloth on the bump on her forehead.

An hour later Justine wrapped herself in a towel and ordered dinner. Logan hadn't called to her. He hadn't even knocked on their adjoining door. She'd fully expected him to insist on taking her to dinner; in fact, she'd gone over several possible refusals while soaking in the tub. Now as she dried her hair and let it fall damply to her shoulders, Justine was just a little irritated that she hadn't had the chance to try them out and test her own reserve. The man kept surprising her.

While she waited for dinner she slipped on her chemise and after shaking them out thoroughly, put on the blouse and fuchsia skirt. She looked at herself in the mirror and decided that what she saw wasn't as bad as she'd expected. Her wild curls were clean and shiny, her face scrubbed and pinkened by a day in the sun on La Quinta. As she examined her face closely she fumbled through her purse for mascara and lipstick.

Justine had never thought of herself as pretty, only passable. Her nose was a little short, her face too round and her top lip almost shapeless, which gave the appearance of a perpetual pout. But her coloring, the dark red hair and brown eyes, saved her, along with the sense of style that had gone into turning Clara Johnson into Justine Hart. Mascara and lipstick helped that image along, but it wouldn't be needed tonight, she thought, and put the cosmetics back into her bag.

The bath, the sea air and later the delicious island dinner gave her a refreshed and vital feeling, along with a sense of loss. When she thought about the adventure she and Logan had shared, Justine realized that she'd enjoyed it. Yet she'd ended it by having dinner alone.

The night breeze came into the room gently, caressed her bare arms and legs and tempted her out onto the balcony. She stepped through the French doors as if drawn by the beckoning hands of the breeze, and at precisely the same moment another door opened, and Logan stood beside her.

"Our rooms share the same balcony, it seems," he said with a look Justine could only call shy. "Don't go away," he added softly.

"I won't," she responded as if to assure him that she wasn't some kind of sprite who would disappear on the breeze. He didn't seem to know just what she was, and she couldn't blame him. Sometimes Justine wasn't sure herself.

"Did you enjoy your dinner?" he asked.

"Yes, did you?"

"Yes, very much," he answered. After a pause he added, tentatively, "Somehow I expected the wild and crazy rock star Justine to be a little more adventurous."

"And I expected the conservative Logan Addison not to be adventurous at all," she responded with a smile that threatened to take his breath away.

"Apparently, we're neither of us what we appear to be."

The moon raced across the sky, pushed, it seemed, by the breeze. "It's a beautiful night," Justine said. "I guess I didn't notice it when we were trudging along."

"No, I guess you didn't." He'd taken off the vest and jacket and rolled up his sleeves. His shirt was unbuttoned halfway down the front. Justine tried to avoid letting her eyes rest on the man standing by her. He had a look that on anyone else would seem merely casual, but on Logan seemed . . . sexual, as if he were wearing no clothes at all, it was such a departure from his usual attire.

She turned her gaze across the sea, listening to the gentle wash of the waves, hearing the breeze in the trees. They stood like that for seconds that turned to minutes, silently side by side in this unusual paradise. Then she mumbled something about finally getting some sleep and started to go back to her room.

She'd half turned away from him when he reached out and took her hand. Logan's grasp was firm, and she caught her breath at the unexpected touch. She looked back at him and saw something in his eyes both challenging and intimate. Confused, she lowered her gaze and at that moment he released her hand. It was over.

Justine went through the door and into her room, still confused by what he'd wanted from her. Any other man would have taken her in his arms if they'd reached the moment of intimacy that she and Logan had reached, at least in their gazes. But he'd released her just when she'd thought he would draw her closer. Again, he'd done what she'd least expected.

Logan watched her go inside, turning out the light as she moved to her bed. He continued to stand there on the balcony for a long time, not thinking of the beauty of the night but of the beauty—and mystery— of the woman.

When he'd reached out for her hand, the sense of adventure that had possessed him all day had risen again, far more powerfully, inside of him. But the gesture had been an impulsive one, and Logan wasn't used to acting impulsively. He hadn't wanted to go any further. He hadn't wanted to become someone reck- lessly accepted by Justine, the fabulous star. He wouldn't have wanted it that way. She was a woman whose mystery should be explored slowly as he learned about her.

Yet in hesitating he'd lost his chance, and that chance was over. Now she was in bed, alone, asleep, her red hair cascading over the pillows. Logan closed his eyes and let the image possess him for an instant. She would have taken off the wild flowered blouse and fuchsia skirt and climbed into bed wearing—what? He tried to imagine the lingerie beneath her clothes. Something lacy and delicate that was just a whisper against her skin, hiding nothing. He could see her firm breasts beneath the lace, the curve of waist and hip as she stretched out on the cool sheets.

Logan shook his head and dislodged the vision but not without smiling wryly to himself. Alone with Justine on a tropical island and he'd let her slip away. Tomorrow it would all be over; tomorrow they'd be on their way home.

Chapter Three

When Justine came down the stairs of the hotel the next morning, she was wearing her red sunglasses again. Logan stepped forward to meet her and was greeted by a tentative smile. The glasses were firmly in place, and Logan realized they were back where they started again. Perhaps that was best. As soon as contact was made with the mainland, they'd be flying back to New York, their adventure in the night only a memory. At least, Logan thought with a hidden smile, it would be a memory for *him*—one that he'd never forget.

"Steve's waiting outside in the courtyard," Logan told her as they walked together across the lobby. Without looking in her direction, he added with just a touch of conspiracy in his voice, "Angelique's with him." He waited for a reaction, and finally Justine smiled.

"The charter company may have saved a plane and lost a pilot," she said.

"Oh, I doubt if it's going to get that serious," Logan responded, but when they stepped out onto the street and saw Steve and Angelique waiting by the fountain, Logan paused for a moment with second thoughts. They looked like teenagers, laughing and flirting, but with a sweetness that was nice to see. As the two couples walked up the steep hill toward the business area of town, Logan began to see signs that, if he hadn't known better, would have made him suspect that Steve and Angelique had known each other for a long time. This didn't look like a one-night stand for the pilot. Already, despite the brief time, it looked serious.

They climbed the hill, Steve and Angelique in front, horsing around, and behind them Logan and a silent Justine. She, too, had been watching the other couple and something akin to jealousy had begun to nag at her. They were enjoying this moment together on a tropical island, making the most of it while she was alternately morose, anxious and confused by what had happened—or hadn't happened—between her and Logan. Somehow she couldn't make her spirits lift. She didn't know whether it was anger she felt or regret.

At the top of the winding hill was a handful of shops including a tiny store packed with clothes to appeal to the tourists, a little grocery and a multipurpose shop belonging to the infamous Martin. The sign hanging in the window declared boldly: FERMÉ.

"Oh, great, it's closed," Justine said with a sigh. Somehow, she'd almost expected to be greeted by another stumbling block. That's the way things had been going and seemed likely to continue.

"Back at ten o'clock," Logan said, translating the sign and then looking at his watch and assuring Justine with what hopefulness he could muster, "That's only five more minutes."

She didn't answer, but Steve was gleeful. "Come on," he said to Angelique. "*Allons*. Let's go next door. I'll buy you something pretty." They ducked into the little clothing shop, where they tarried and had to be fetched by Logan when, twenty minutes later, Martin finally arrived.

The foursome followed the little man into his shop while Logan explained their purpose. Martin, like most of the others on St. Cat's, spoke a very basic English, enough to be understood by the tourists.

"Come this way," he said, leading them through a maze of items, including the sandals made by Monsieur Moreau, which sold, Justine noted without surprise, for less than Logan had paid. Such necessities as automobile tires, alarm clocks and magazines from the States, several weeks old, lined the walls of his shop.

"Here it is," Martin said proudly as they reached the back of the store. The large multiband radio with earphones and speakers looked impressive. However, they quickly discovered that it was broken.

"What?" Justine was nonplussed by the news, wondering why in the world the little man had dragged them all the way through the shop to proudly show off his radio when it didn't even work.

To be sure that he got the facts right, Logan questioned Martin carefully in French and then translated for the others. "The radio went on the blink last week, apparently, and he's ordered a new part..."

Justine opened her mouth to speak, thought better of it and let Logan continue.

"The replacement will arrive on the next mail boat..."

Again Justine waited. Logan knew what she wanted to say, and he also knew how she would react to the next rather vague news.

"...which will arrive tomorrow," he said, "or—the next day." He didn't even bother to look in Justine's direction. He could well imagine the look on her face.

"Can you be a little more specific?" Justine asked the man directly, only to receive a blank stare.

"One day or two?" Logan simplified.

Martin shrugged. "Possibly one, possibly two. This is St. Cat's," he said as if that explained everything. "It will come when it will come. No problem," he added, using the term most often thrown at tourists, which immediately made Justine wince.

"Time to enjoy life," he declared sagely.

"Not a bad philosophy," Logan found himself muttering.

Justine, without even vaguely echoing those sentiments, spoke to the man slowly and carefully, pausing between each word. "Please, let us know when the boat arrives." She pointed down the hill. "We are at the inn."

Martin laughed, his narrow shoulders shaking. "Everyone will know when the mail boat comes. This is the most big event on St. Cat's. The captain will blow his whistle, and everyone will come running. You wait.''

Steve had stopped listening and was wandering through the shop with Angelique, looking for something "pretty" to buy her. Nothing appealed to him so he waved a casual goodbye to Justine and Logan and, taking Angelique by the hand, headed out the door. "We'll see you later—maybe," he told them with a grin.

Logan thanked the shop's fun-loving owner, and Justine forced a smile, reminding him again that they would be at the inn—waiting—when the radio was put in working order.

Out on the street, they discovered that morning had finally awakened the sleepy town. A few islanders had set up stalls shaded by big umbrellas in the open air and had begun calling out their wares. Another couple from the inn—Swiss or possibly German, Justine decided—was already rummaging through the items for sale, and a few others who were dressed like tourists appeared with their wallets, ready to buy. The bustle centered around a one-block area. Everywhere else it was quiet, the only noise the buzz of bees around the flowers.

Even in the lovely courtyard beside the inn, which they could see from atop the hill, everything was quiet and peaceful, almost lazily so. Justine breathed in the scent of flowers and felt herself begin to relax. But she was still frustrated enough with the circumstances of their isolation to get in one more verbal dig. It was said with something of a pout but not very seriously meant. "Maybe we could hitch a ride on the mythical mail boat."

Logan laughed. "And hop around the islands for the next week or so? No, we're better off waiting and taking it easy," he added, actually stretching, which Justine thought was carrying things a little too far. "We have all day," he drawled.

"And tomorrow, too," Justine reminded him. "Maybe even the next day."

Logan smiled. "Don't fight it, Justine. We're here, and there's not a damn thing we can do until what you call the mythical boat arrives. I suggest we follow the lead of Steve and Angelique—kick back and enjoy ourselves."

They'd stopped beside a low stone wall that enclosed a field, where a few straggly goats grazed. Beyond them was another perfect view of the island and the sea. Justine sat down on the wall. "But don't you feel powerless?" she asked.

"There's nothing we can do," Logan answered as he sat down beside her, "until the indomitable Martin gets his radio fixed."

"And by then they'll be frantic back in New York, Frank and all my staff. They'll think we crashed, Logan, they'll think—"

"But imagine how happy they'll be when they find out we're alive and well!" He smiled boyishly at her, and as she had been all along, Justine was charmed. "Imagine the fun the tabloids will have with this one: 'The famous Justine discovered on a tropical island with her dashing financial advisor.'"

Justine groaned. "I'd forgotten all about the press. More publicity is just what I don't want right now."

"There's nothing we can do about it," Logan reminded her again, to Justine's irritation.

"I know, I know," she said, "but I don't need to keep hearing it."

"Then don't keep complaining," Logan said with a smile that softened the suggestion, "and let's do some shopping. Personally, I'm getting a little tired of these clothes," he said, "and as much as I liked your outfit in the beginning, I must admit it looks a little strange with sandals."

Justine couldn't help laughing. "I know. I feel like a total fool."

"Then let's buy you something more suitable for the islands. Since we have to stay here for a while."

"Please, Logan," she said, taking his hand as he helped her up, "don't rub it in."

In addition to the clothing store, there were carts under the umbrellas with all the necessary beach accoutrements. Logan stopped at the first stall and held up a pink T-shirt that looked about two sizes too small. "Could you squeeze into this?"

Justine raised one eyebrow but didn't comment, and Logan reminded himself that the remark was too familiar, not very smart at a time when Justine was just beginning to relax. He cursed himself silently, adding, "Whatever you decide to buy, remember, it's on Norwood and Addison."

She pulled down the red sunglasses until they rested on the top of her nose and looked at him over the rims for a long minute before saying, "You're on. And don't tell me I didn't warn you."

Justine began seriously looking through the clothes, calling out to him over her shoulder, "Do you plan just to watch, or are *you* included on this expense account, too?"

"I'm included," he answered.

"I can't wait to see what you buy, since there don't seem to be any three-piece suits here."

"Well, I'll just have to change my image," came the reply. But Justine was already into her spree, picking up bathing suits, shorts, T-shirts and "a dress for dinner," she said out loud but not within his earshot. She'd already decided not to sulk in her room tonight.

An hour later Logan was back at the wall, sitting in the sun, waiting. He'd changed into a pair of white shorts and a T-shirt emblazoned with *St. Cat's* in bold but slightly crooked red letters and a pair of Monsieur Moreau's sandals. He'd also bought a bathing suit and a beach towel, long cotton pants and a flowered shirt, having taken her remark about three-piece suits seriously.

Another hour passed before Justine joined him, her arms full of packages, which Logan didn't even notice. He was looking at *her*, seeing more of Justine Hart than he'd ever seen, just about as much as he'd imagined. She was wearing a pair of flimsy striped shorts and, he could have sworn, the very same T-shirt he'd tempted her with. Her legs were just as long as he'd speculated from the strides that had kept her in step with him. Logan tried not to stare.

"I guess I overdid it," Justine said with a radiant smile as Logan relieved her of some of the packages.

He ignored the remark, commenting, "I can't wait to see what's in the other packages. If it's anything like what you have on . . ."

Justine smiled slyly. "Actually, I bought a bathing suit and another T-shirt and a sundress and—" She stopped for a moment and then reminded him, "One package contains the clothes I had on, so it's not *all* new purchases."

"Don't apologize," he said as they started back down the hill toward the inn. "I gave you carte blanche, so I'm to blame." Logan had almost gotten used to the way she looked in the shorts and T-shirt. Almost, but not quite.

The sun was beginning to beat down on them, and Justine opened one of her packages to fish out a big floppy hat that she deposited on top of her curls. The brim almost covered her eyes.

"Maybe you can take off your sunglasses now," Logan suggested.

"Maybe," she answered, making no move to comply. "What's next?"

"Getting into our bathing suits, grabbing a lounge chair under a palm tree, ordering rum punch and vegetating for the rest of the day. Or is that too boring for Justine Hart?"

He waited for her answer as they went through the lobby of the inn and climbed the stairs to the second floor, where they stopped to look out the back window. Below them through a path of oleander, the white sand stretched toward a bright blue sea. "Ymm," she said a little hedonistically, "I can't wait for the boredom to begin. Do you know when I last had a vacation?"

He shook his head.

"Neither do I!" she said. "I'm not sure I've really ever had one, except for an occasional day in exotic places between concerts, and that usually dwindled to an hour or so because of rehearsals. No," she decided, shaking her head, "I don't think I've had a real vacation since it all began." And not before that, either, Justine thought to herself. The summers in Georgia had been spent working, too, at one tacky job after another all through high school. "Now I'm ready. Let's vacation!" she said, opening the door to her room and falling in with her packages and the ones Logan handed over to her. "I'll meet you at the beach."

Four hours and two rum punches later, Justine opened her eyes, looked around and reluctantly stood up, wiping the sand from the front of her legs. She'd been lying on her stomach long enough she decided lazily. Time to climb back into the deck chair. She dug a hole in the shade cast by the canvas sling, put her glass in it and collapsed into the chair. Her eyes stayed open long enough to appreciate the setting once more—for the tenth time that afternoon.

Tall spiky palm trees grew along the beach like bony sentinels marching through floral beds to stop just at the edge of the white sand where they swayed with sybaritic ease amid the profusion of flowers. The scents wafted across the sand toward Justine and blended with sounds of laughter that were almost musical.

Lazily, Justine turned her head toward the noise. The little fishing fleet was coming in. Blue and white boats freshly painted and bearing romantic French names raced atop the waves and came to shore, the force of the current hurling them several yards clear of the water. The owners, stripped to the waist and wearing brightly colored pants and high boots jumped out to secure their boats. Then they joined their mates who'd already settled in the cove mending nets and baiting lines for the next day's catch. They called out to one another as they worked, the quality of their speech as melodic as the songs that soon followed.

Far out on the rickety wooden pier, another voice, higher pitched and almost demanding, sang out her wares of bananas and coconuts and pineapples. Squinting against the sun, Justine could see the large woman in a flowered dress move with a slow undulating gait along the pier, pushing her cart filled with fruit. Her voice faded as she reached the far end of the pier and then grew stronger as she turned and retraced her steps.

Justine, lulled by the sounds and by the scented breeze, sipped her rum punch and tried not to let her eyes close. Turning in her chair slightly to follow the sun, she looked north, where the beach angled sharply. Huge rocks jutted out into the water, and the white sand narrowed to a ribbon-thin strip that seemed to race between the rocks, appearing and disappearing until it ended at a jagged curve in the beach. Idly Justine contemplated about what was around that curve. She wondered if she and Logan would walk north along the beach, climb the rocks and explore the unseen island that lay beyond her view.

She hesitated halfway through the thought, catching herself in an expression that had buzzed through her head all morning like the bees around the bougainvillea. *She and Logan.* She'd been thinking of them as a pair, a couple, a twosome here together as if on a planned vacation, when in reality their time on St. Cat's was nothing of the sort. An act of fate had stranded them here. But Justine couldn't complain. If she had to be stranded with someone, Logan Addison wasn't a bad choice. Once she'd gotten over his infuriatingly philosophical way of looking at everything—particularly infuriating since Justine had finally had to admit to herself that it was right—there was no way to control what was happening to them.

She planned to enjoy it up to a point. But because the setting was so tropically lush and because Logan had adapted so well to the environment, becoming a figure as romantic as the place itself, she'd have to be careful. Things were different here, easier, more tempting. She mustn't forget that the good-looking man with whom she'd spent a morning on the beach was her financial advisor, not her leading man in a romantic saga in paradise.

Justine was realistic enough to know that. She'd been very much in control of her life, and everyone in it, since Brady. She'd learned the importance of keeping control during those days, and she wasn't about to forget it. Yet lying in the sun with songs and laughter and a warm scented breeze to caress her, her vow to stay in control didn't seem very important. It drifted in and out of her mind only to be swept away on the tide and forgotten.

She felt his shadow block out the sun and cool her hot skin, and she knew he was standing over her before he spoke, before she opened her eyes to see him. She smiled secretly, pleased to be so sure that it was Logan.

"You look comfortable."

She opened her eyes and looked up at him. "I am," she commented softly. "Where've you been?" Even in her reverie, she'd missed him there beside her.

"Reconnoitering." Logan dropped several magazines on her lap. "Not the latest issues, but they're more current than the ones our friend Martin sells in his shop."

Justine looked at the magazines idly and then put them aside. "Later, maybe..." she said in a voice so lazy that it didn't quite complete the words.

Logan laughed and sat down on the beach towel beside her, reaching for her hat, which had fallen from the back of the chair. He shook the sand off it and placed it unceremoniously on top of her curls. "This sun can be dangerous, and your skin is very fair."

"I've been turning every half hour."

"Like a chicken on a spit," he reminded her, "which eventually gets well done all over. On humans it's called sunburn," he added.

"I'm tougher than I look," was Justine's immediate response.

Logan looked over at her with a little frown. "Well, keep the hat on just the same," he advised her, and for some reason she didn't object, pulling the wide brim down over her eyes, causing Logan to observe that between the floppy hat and the huge sunglasses, her face was certainly well protected from the sun, and from his admiring gaze, as well. But the rest of her was in full view, and he looked, as he'd been looking all day, at the long-legged Justine Hart, clad in a green bikini that hid just enough of her ivory skin to make the two pieces of material qualify as a bathing suit. He'd examined every inch available to his view and imagined the rest a dozen times. He'd memorized the curve of her long leg and rounded hip, the flat stomach, now slightly pinkened by the sun. He'd even mentally counted the few delicious freckles that the sun had scattered across her chest beneath the touch of tan.

Shaking away his erotic thoughts, Logan stood up. "I'm going in," he said, and she watched carefully as he stretched, his long muscles flexing in the sun. "Want to join me? The water's like silk."

Justine shook her head, still a little too relaxed, if not too lazy, to move. "I'll cool off later," she said.

His shrug seemed unconcerned, or so he hoped. Logan was still aching to get her into the water beside him if only to see how the bikini would cling to her when it got wet, whether the top would slip down a little, revealing another inch of her creamy breasts or whether the cold water would harden her nipples beneath the flimsy material. Logan shook his head as he entered the water. He'd better stop thinking like that, he told himself, or he was going to need this cooling swim more than a few times during the rest of the day.

Justine had arranged the floppy hat so she could see Logan walk away from her toward the sea. She wasn't really surprised by what she saw. Under the three-piece suits she'd known there was a good build but, like the adventurous part of his personality, it was better than she'd expected. She'd known Logan couldn't always be so coolly perfect, but the depth and variety of his character had taken her unawares. So had his body.

It wasn't overly muscular, but when he walked away from her into the water, the muscles rippled everywhere, in his long legs, across his broad back and upper arms and wide shoulders. They were muscles held in check, rippling but not bulging, long and lean...and perfectly beautiful. He waded in up to his hips and then dived out and under an approaching wave. Justine looked away and picked up one of the magazines, flipping disinterestedly through it. Soon her eyes strayed back to the azure water to see his dark head glistening, his arms stretched out in front as he caught a wave and rode it halfway to shore, turned, dived again and emerged, shaking his hair free of water, waiting for the surf to build again. He was a man full of energy. In New York the energy was released on a squash court. Here, through long walks on the beach and riding the waves.

Justine continued to watch as he swam far out beyond the breakers and, finally, took one last, large wave to shore. Behind all her sunscreen paraphernalia, she knew Logan couldn't see that she was following his every move, but she was. She watched him stop near her chair and pick up his towel, watched him shake the last drops of water from his black hair and towel it off. She watched without changing the tilt of her head, all while surreptitiously reading a magazine. She didn't even know which one.

His broad chest was slightly matted with dark hair. His stomach muscles were flat and hard, and a line of dark hair ran from below his navel and disappeared under his bathing suit. Justine's eyes stopped there as she tried to ignore the way the wet suit clung to his hips, tried to ignore the manly curve that the suit wouldn't let her ignore. Then, thankfully, he turned away, dried his back and legs and dropped into a chair beside her.

"The water is fantastic, but I told you that before, didn't I?" He smiled apologetically. "I don't mean to wax so enthusiastically about St. Cat's, but you must admit..."

"It's gorgeous," Justine finished. "I've finally become convinced, and I've decided to stay." Logan laughed. "And enjoy it," she added.

"Good," he mumbled as he leaned back in his chair and closed his eyes.

But Justine was still watching him, blatantly now that his eyes were closed. His perfunctory toweling hadn't completely done the job. His chest was still wet, the dark hair damply curled. She wondered what it would be like to touch his chest, run her fingers through the coal-black hair, move her hands upward to his neck and across his shoulders and down his arm, caressing the skin.

What, she wondered, would his skin feel like to her touch? Suddenly she knew, it would be soft and hard at the same time, tender on the surface and tough beneath, silk over steel, and it would radiate heat and energy and life. Touching him would be like touching a flame, warm and living and strong. Justine was suddenly afraid, and yet at the same time she was curious, so curious to know. She wanted to reach out now and...

Then she realized that he was awake. Adjusting her hat carefully, Justine could look into his eyes. What she saw there caused a warm glow to spread through her, heating her from within, warming every fiber of her being just as the sun warmed the surface of her tingling skin.

As she let herself melt into those feelings, Justine became suddenly afraid that he *could* see her, that he could tell what was happening behind her hat and her glasses, what feelings were mirrored in her eyes. She felt a blush rising in her cheeks and quickly looked away, chiding herself for fantasizing about Logan Addison. It was as if she'd never seen a man quite as good-looking as Logan now that he'd shed the suit and conservative manner that went with it. Yes, she'd decided, he was extremely attractive in every way.

Brady had been good-looking, too, she remembered with a jolt, warning herself not to get led on, not to get fooled and especially not to mix these emotions she was feeling with the behavior that had always existed and should—would—continue to exist between her and her business advisor.

She remembered the unexpected jolt that had come over her the night before when he'd stepped out onto the balcony, freed from the trappings of a financier, his sleeves rolled up and his shirt unbuttoned, becoming, for the first time, Logan, the man. That had been just a hint of what was to come as they moved together through this idyll, which would soon end, Justine told herself. She tried to remember how anxiously she'd been awaiting the arrival of the mail boat. Yet she hadn't thought of it all afternoon and right this moment didn't care if it never came.

All during the day and into the evening, she tried to think not of fantasy, but of the reality that was personified in the mail boat—which still hadn't arrived. But even if she wasn't going to give herself over to the romance of St. Cat's, it would be ridiculous to eat in her room alone again. After sharing the day, she and Logan could certainly share dinner.

They did, amid the bustle and bright confusion of a wedding party. The hotel restaurant was filled with islanders, eating and drinking and spilling out onto the patio where, to the beat of an energetic trio, they danced. Steve and Angelique were among the guests, celebrating with the same gay intensity. Yet even among the crowd they only had eyes for each other.

Justine and Logan sat at a corner table, gave up trying to talk and dined quickly so they could retreat to the relative quiet of a little café across the lobby, where only a handful of the wedding party had wandered. There they sat at a table in the corner and ordered coffee to end the evening.

"Good choice," Logan said.

"Yes," Justine agreed, looking around with relief at the quiet group in the café.

"That's not what I meant."

Justine looked at him quizzically.

"I'm talking about your dress. It was a good choice." The dress was creamy white with an embroidered scooped neck and very simple lines. "It suits you," he said quietly, and Justine felt herself blush. "You look more beautiful than ever, if that's possible."

"I didn't even put on any makeup tonight," Justine admitted, not quite sure why she chose to tell him that. "I believe it's a first for Justine Hart—after sundown, anyway."

Logan laughed and thought about how fresh and young she looked without makeup, not like a star at all.

She was having similar thoughts. "It's a good thing none of my fans are here to see me out of character like this," she said. "We all have our images to protect. Even Logan Addison."

"Especially Logan Addison. My clients want to have faith in their advisors, who must be forthright and honorable. And square," he added.

Justine laughed. "Well, maybe careful is a better word." She looked at him steadily. "Are you all of those things, or is that Logan Addison the image and this the real one?"

"I hope that I'm a combination of both—a good businessman with a sense of adventure. I don't always admit it to myself—in fact, I almost never do—but I like to take chances and explore unknown territory. I guess I like danger," he added. "I'm not afraid, Justine." His eyes met hers directly.

After a fleeting second she looked away, and Logan cursed himself for being too obvious. Every time he skirted the edges of intimacy, she moved back, retreated from him, if not physically then emotionally. At least she wasn't hiding behind those damned glasses tonight. He could be sure now when she felt uneasy, be sure when he'd overstepped and then have the sense to draw back. As much as he wanted her, he wouldn't make a move until he had some sign from her. Without the glasses, he would be able to see the sign. But it hadn't come yet; he had the feeling it would be a long time coming.

That was as it should be, he decided. They needed more time to learn about each other. He needed to *know* her. He had no idea how long that would take, but her next remark gave him the chance to begin, at least to tell her something about himself.

"You and Frank are so different," she said. "I've often wondered how you got into business together."

That was his opening, and he took it. "We knew each other in college and were pretty good friends. But right after I graduated I took the obvious course and went into the family firm."

"The family firm," she said, a little in awe. "That sounds so stable. Years and years of New England aristocracy."

He nodded. "Established, I suspect, by a robber-baron type and then brought to respectability over the years. Anyway, the investments my family handled were good and solid, just like the firm. I thought they were fine for me until Frank offered me something more interesting, and challenging. Then I realized how bored I'd really been. I left in the midst of an uproar with my father reminding me that no Addison had ever worked with 'theatrical' people!"

Justine laughed. "Do they think you've become contaminated?"

"No, they've finally accepted my decision, more or less. I'm always welcome to return to the fold, but there's not a chance I'd ever go back—not with clients like mine."

He couldn't help it. He reached out and touched her hand. It was small and soft and cool in his. He wanted to do more than touch her there. He wanted to move his hand up the smooth skin of her arm and touch her shoulder, her long slim neck. He wanted to touch the fullness of her breast and hold her.

But she'd moved her hand away. The silence that followed was awkward, and he tried to fill it. "I must be boring you with my life story."

The look in her brown eyes was honest. "Not at all. I've wondered about you and Frank. You make such a good team. That's a rarity, isn't it, finding someone you can work well with and trust?"

"It is," he agreed.

The silence between them was repeated around the room and through the hotel. Sometime while they'd talked the wedding party had left, moved on down the beach, taking the band with them. A few couples, tourists like themselves, remained in the little café. Someone put a coin in the jukebox, and a familiar melody drifted across the room.

"'Summer Masquerade,'" Logan said, "one of my favorite Justine Hart songs."

"It was a big hit for me," she remembered. "My breakout song, as much Broadway melody as rock."

"Yes," he agreed. "I like hearing it on a jukebox in St. Cat's. Come on, let's dance."

"Here?" The room was very small and not meant for dancing.

"Why not? The wedding party was dancing in the restaurant, for Lord's sake," Logan said with a grin as he reached for her hand and took her into his arms before she could think of a response.

Then he was holding her as he'd imagined holding her. She was really in his arms, and he could feel the softness of her skin that was so much softer than he'd believed possible. Her red curls brushed against his chin, and he fought off the desire to fill his hands with her hair and turn her face upward so that he could bend to kiss her lips. Instead he held her gently so that their bodies barely touched and inhaled the sweet fragrance of Justine as her voice sang on the jukebox.

Summer masquerade...
The games we played...
The plans we made...

"This is really amazing," Logan said, "dancing with *you* while Justine sings. Pretty heady stuff."

"I think you may be talking images again," she said, and in her voice he heard a little uneasiness.

Quickly he tried to reassure her. "I'm not holding an image, I'm holding a real woman." And he was. As his arms imperceptibly tightened around her, he could feel the rhythm of her heartbeat, the quickening of her breath. Deep within himself he could feel the primeval stirring that was a need for her, which he'd fought since the night before. He envisioned Justine on the balcony, her skin glowing, her hair still wet from the shower—and then today, Justine on the beach in that barely there bikini—and now, Justine in his arms, her fair skin kissed by the sunlight, fresh and fragrant, all moonglow and candlelight.

Yet he didn't know her. He held her in his arms, but as she'd said, he only held her image. He wanted more.

"Justine—"

"Logan—"

They spoke at the same time. "You first," she said.

"No, you."

"I was just thinking how nice the day has been, how much I enjoyed it after my near-rebellion. And to-night—I enjoyed that, too."

The song had ended, and now there was only her voice, the voice of the woman in his arms. The voice, and the woman, were his for this moment. The thought made him ache with longing, aware of her as a woman and of his need for her as a man. He felt it more deeply now than the night before because he knew now what she looked like beneath the pure-white dress. He didn't have to imagine the swell of her breast, the curve of her thigh.

He also knew the evening was about to end, and he was going to let it end. He could take her to her room, kiss her, hold her and perhaps even make love to her, but something kept him from insisting. He didn't want to have her for a brief time, only to lose her. He would wait.

"The sun's sapped all of my energy," Justine murmured against his chest. "I think it's time for me to turn in."

He'd expected that, and he was convinced he could let her go. Yet he found himself holding her a little more firmly, looking into her face and finding more than exhaustion there. He found another expression that he couldn't quite interpret. It might have been confusion or even fear. "I'll take you up to the room," he said, and waited for her to make the decision for both of them.

She withdrew a little from his arms, and as she stepped away, he reminded himself that he'd promised to let her go. "You stay and have another drink," she said. "I'll see you in the morning."

He let her go. They still had tomorrow...if the boat didn't come.

Chapter Four

Justine always slept late, often until noon, so when she awoke early the next morning, she automatically closed her eyes and turned over, expecting to go back to sleep instantly. She didn't. After she finally gave up and rolled out of bed, Justine realized why. The habit of sleeping late, like the wild clothes, the makeup and the huge red sunglasses, belonged to Justine Hart, the international star. And she didn't feel like that Justine today.

She pulled on a pair of yellow cotton shorts and, slipping a T-shirt over her head, walked out onto the balcony. The sun was just rising over the sea, turning the whole world a pearly pink. It was a gentle sunrise, not a startling one. It crept, the luminescent ball gently emerging from below the horizon like a balloon released on a windless day, slowly climbing into the sky.

Justine couldn't remember when she'd last seen the sunrise, probably not since she was a teenager going off to work early in the morning and hardly noticing the sun coming up over the red dirt fields of Georgia. St. Cat's was certainly presenting Justine with a series of "firsts" or at least "can't remember whens." She was enjoying them all thoroughly.

Most of the enjoyment, Justine realized, came from being with Logan. She shook her head in sheer disbelief, not just that they'd found themselves stranded on this island but that they were enjoying themselves so completely. They were. Yesterday, by the time she'd finally resigned herself to her situation, had been a perfect day in the sun. Last night, too, had been perfect, even though it had ended abruptly, as though in midchapter.

Justine looked across the balcony to the beach and decided that it was time for a walk. She went down the balcony stairs quietly, careful not to wake Logan, whose blinds were still drawn. She could imagine him stretched out on the bed, maybe with one arm thrown over his head, sleeping heavily. She wondered if he slept in the nude. He might have pulled the sheet up over his naked body, or he might have left it rumpled at his feet.

As Justine stepped onto the sand, she was still thinking about his tanned naked body stretched out on the white sheets. Then she began to think back to the night before and the way it ended and how it could have been different.

Justine walked along in the sand that was tinted with a pinkish blush from the rising sun and considered that ending, knowing he'd left it up to her to decide what it would be. She hadn't so much decided as let the decision happen for them. She'd left because it had been late and she'd been tired, but she'd left alone. *That* had been her choice.

He could have insisted on going upstairs with her, or he could have followed a little later. He could have pressed his advantage, but he didn't. That had surprised Justine, and in a warm touching way, it had pleased her. He was a nice man, a decent man. She'd never known anyone like him. Another first, she thought with a smile. The very sweetness of Logan was in itself an overpowering attraction, making her wonder more and more about him. He was intriguing, a mystery, and one she wanted very much to solve.

Justine scattered a flock of gulls that was obviously unprepared for a stranger invading the privacy of the beach so early in the morning. They flew around wildly before resettling in their original places on the beach as soon as she passed. But that little interval hadn't disrupted her thoughts about Logan. He was still very much in her mind.

The mail boat should come today, she knew, but what if it didn't? Their habit of ending their evenings so tentatively and puzzlingly was going to be strained if they had to do it for a third night. She considered not seeing him at all today until the boat arrived. Otherwise, she knew that she might have trouble walking away again because she liked him. She couldn't deny that. To let their relationship change into something more serious would be dangerous, not just because he was her business advisor but because they were of two different worlds. What might happen here would be over as soon as they returned to

New York. Once there, he'd climb back into his three-piece suit, and she would be Justine again. That's the way it was and the way it always would remain.

As she turned and retraced her steps, once more disturbing the gulls, Justine was resolved. She'd keep to herself today. Any other choice would be very, very wrong. She wasn't about to get involved again with a man who handled her money. She'd put first things first and let him make the deal for La Quinta. As for the rest, she'd continue to carefully compartmentalize her life, and she'd keep her distance.

Making the resolution, she found as she approached the inn, was easy. Putting Logan out of her mind was impossible. If only he weren't so nice *and* so exciting. That was a combination that Justine had never encountered, and it was an intriguing one. She felt herself shivering a bit in the now-warming sun, just thinking about him. That disturbed her and made her resolve even more firm.

Logan broke through it almost immediately. He was sitting on the balcony at a wrought-iron-and-glass table that had been set up between their two rooms. The scent of strong coffee and pastries drifted toward her on the breeze. She'd thought of going around to the front of the inn, trying to avoid him, but he'd already seen her and was waving her forward.

"Time for breakfast," he called out.

Well, just breakfast, Justine decided, since there really was no way she could avoid it now. Besides, the aromas were very tempting. So, she admitted, was Logan, standing up now to greet her, wearing the blue flowered shirt and white pants he'd bought the day before. His hair was still damp from a shower, and his eyes sparkled with a kind of early morning joy that gladdened Justine's heart. This was going to be difficult, she admitted.

Logan pulled out a chair for her, and Justine sat down, not without noticing the clean fresh scent of him, which wasn't soap or cologne, just a freshness that was Logan. Combined with the breakfast odors, it was all just about too much for Justine. Her head spun a little as she sat down, famished, and took a big bite of her croissant. It was buttery and delicious. Logan certainly knew how to win a hungry girl's heart.

"Did you enjoy your walk?"

Justine, sipping her coffee, could only nod.

"The news around the inn is that there's a good chance the mail boat will arrive this afternoon," he informed her as he poured himself some more coffee. "So I thought maybe we should make the most of this morning."

Justine listened, prepared to refuse whatever he tempted her with. He was definitely going to tempt her. His face lit up boyishly. "My idea is pretty appealing, I think. I bet you'll agree. Now listen." He leaned forward almost conspiratorially. "The inn owns an old Jeep. I'm pretty sure I can talk them into lending it to us. We can have that tour of the island we thought about yesterday but were too lazy to follow through with."

"Logan, I don't think—"

He frowned briefly and imperceptibly but didn't pause long enough to let her refuse. "Why not?" he forced, knowing there wasn't a logical reason.

There wasn't. As firmly as she'd been resolved to stay away from him today, she couldn't even think of

an excuse. If she'd really *wanted* to refuse his offer of
a tour of the island, she could simply have stood up,
said *no thank you*, and gone to her room. But they'd
passed that point a long time ago, passed the point
when she could treat their relationship as if it were new
and stilted. It wasn't. Still, she couldn't agree to his
plan.

"I'm told there's a lagoon to the north," he said,
tempting her with visions of what was around that
bend in the beach she'd wondered about. He reached
over and put his hand on her arm. She could feel the
warmth in his touch, and it brought back the memories of last night. Justine knew she was in trouble.

Logan didn't hesitate. "They'll pack a lunch for us,
and we can just take off—go anywhere we want to.
When was the last time you did that?"

Oh, God, Justine thought, she was being con-
fronted with *another* first. "Never," she answered. "I
don't think I ever had a *planned* picnic on a lagoon,
much less an impromptu one." She was hooked, and
she didn't care. So much for resolve. It was a beautiful morning, and she couldn't think of anything that
would be more fun than spending it with Logan.

"So there," he said, even though she hadn't really
answered. "We'll go off with no destination, no time-
table, free and easy. What could be better?"

"Nothing could be better," she said, and meant it.

The Jeep performed rather unwillingly, Justine
thought, on the hills along the coast, heading north
with a reluctant sputter as they climbed and then
something akin to a sigh as they descended. The wind
caught in Justine's hair and tangled her curls. As had

become her habit here, she wasn't wearing makeup, and she felt like a kid, squealing with delight as the Jeep plunged down yet another hill, and laughed as Logan was laughing at the sheer joy of being free in the mountains of the island.

They passed one other vehicle, an old truck hauling fruit and vegetables to town. Deep in a valley, a young boy almost aimlessly herded his goats. Nothing was rushed. Time seemed to move as slowly as the pace, seconds turning into minutes, minutes into hours in such a leisurely fashion that Justine thought the day might never end. That would be all right with her, spending an endless day with a man who was, she'd decided, the only man who could have completed the scene. He belonged here just as Justine did, and yet she would never have imagined either of them fitting in. They weren't the types for this kind of life.

"Maybe St. Cat's weaves some kind of magical spell that changes everyone who comes here," she said aloud.

Logan glanced over at her, put the Jeep into high gear, stepped on the gas and roared down the hill. "I've considered that possibility," he said. "And I wonder if it's a permanent change. When we get back to New York, will we take our love for lazy days with us or will we get right into the rat race with the same dedication as before?"

"Unfortunately, we don't have much choice. Our careers—"

"Yes, our careers," Logan interrupted, knowing that they both were avid workers and loved what they did for a living. Neither of them could give up what they had worked so hard for, not for anything, not even for this. "But we won't forget," he said.

"No," Justine repeated. "We'll never forget."

"Look," Logan called out suddenly, "there's the lagoon."

It was an inland bay, bright blue near the shore, turquoise and indigo beyond the reefs, calm, without the ripple of a wave. "This must be the road leading down to it," Logan said, turning onto a rocky, rutted road. "Reminds me of our trip from the airstrip to town." Looking over at her with a twinkle in his eye, he asked, "Remember?"

Justine groaned. "That's something I'll never forget either! At least this time we don't have to walk," she said as the Jeep plowed along the road until they reached the bottom and the lagoon stretched before them. The sand, just as white as on the main beaches, was a narrow strip here, separating the water from a mass of jungle at the edge of which someone had constructed a little lean-to of palm fronds. "Perfect," Justine said as they got out of the Jeep carrying the picnic basket and towels with them.

"First a swim," Logan decided, putting down all the paraphernalia. "And this time, I'm going to get you into the water."

"I went in yesterday," she reminded him.

"Yes, while I was off on a walk. I want you out there with me."

"But I can't swim." Justine reminded him of what she'd finally admitted the day before.

"I'll teach you," he declared, stripping off his clothes and standing in front of her in his bathing suit.

"And if that fails, you can just float. The salt water will hold you up. Come on," he insisted.

Justine still stood in the shade of the lean-to, a little shyly, not quite ready to take off her shorts and T-shirt in front of him, even though she wore the bikini he'd seen the day before beneath her clothes. There was something too personal about undressing while Logan watched. "You go on," she suggested. "I'll be right behind you."

"Promise?"

"Promise." She watched him turn and run across the narrow strip of sand to the water. He didn't slow down as he splashed into the lagoon but kept running as far as he could until the water reached his bathing suit and he stretched into a dive, disappearing and then reappearing, turning and calling out to her. She'd been so mesmerized as he swam that Justine still hadn't taken off her clothes and would have to undress with Logan watching after all. Well, she thought, at least he wasn't standing right beside her.

Quickly, she was ready to take her plunge. She made her way into the water less enthusiastically than Logan, however, shivering a little at the initial shock of the cold and then as she ventured out farther, getting used to the temperature. There were no waves, but Justine still would only venture waist high, sink down, let the cool water come to her shoulders and quickly get back up, standing with feet embedded deep in the sand for security.

"Ready for your lesson?" Logan asked as he swam up to her.

Justine shook her head. "I think it's a little late for me to learn to swim. Maybe you could teach me something simple like how to float."

Logan laughed. "You're on." He reached out and suddenly she was in his arms.

"Logan!"

"Relax." He tried not to look at the two strips of green bikini. Now that they were wet, nothing was left to the imagination, and just as he'd thought it might, the top of her suit had slipped enough to reveal the edge of one pink nipple. She tugged at the strap but too late. "Now, stretch out," he said hoarsely, trying to keep his mind on the promised lesson.

Justine did as she was told, but her body was rigid.

"I've got you, so don't worry. Just let everything go limp."

She tried to relax, but it wasn't fear of the water that made relaxing impossible. One of his hands was on the small of her back, and the other was under her thighs, right at the line of her buttocks where her bathing suit should have been, but wasn't.

The bottom of her bikini had ridden up in the water, and Logan could feel his hand on that tempting indentation between thigh and hip. He could also feel her tenseness and knew he was the cause of it. After a few more delicious seconds, he moved his hand down her thigh and felt her relax. Moments later she was floating.

"I told you it was easy," he said when the lesson ended. She jackknifed her body until once more her feet were touching the sand and she was standing beside him. "Swimming lessons come later," he added, leading her back to shore. "You're a good pupil. Now tell me why in the world, *how* in the world, you managed to avoid learning to swim?''

"I don't know. I just never learned." He'd stopped and picked up a towel. Carefully, without touching her flesh with his hand, Logan dried Justine's back and waited for her to explain.

When she remained silent, he asked, "Were you afraid?''

"Oh, no," she denied. "There was just never a chance. Besides, I didn't have a place to swim. We didn't belong to a club or anything. We were very poor," she said quickly.

Logan knew he'd touched a nerve, and he wanted to find out more about what caused the tenderness there. Yet he didn't want to push, knowing that this was the beginning of getting to know Justine. He'd need to move slowly, at her own pace. "Well," he said softly, "I guess a girl can't be beautiful and a good swimmer, too, that's probably asking too much."

"I'm not beautiful, either," Justine said suddenly. "I've never been beautiful."

Logan stopped drying her back and wrapped the towel around her, letting her tuck it in front. "I've never known anyone more beautiful." He was still standing behind her, and Justine didn't turn around to look at him when she answered.

"That's just the *image* you're talking about, the glamour, the aura, the style, all that. But not me."

He touched her shoulder gently and turned her around. "I'm not looking at the image now, Justine."

She stepped away and absently began to unpack the lunch basket, spreading a plaid tablecloth on the sand under the palm-frond roof. "I've known ever since I was a child that I was plain," she said. "My face is too round, my upper lip is too full, my—"

Logan was laughing. "Keep going. You're naming all your loveliest features."

"My hair..."

He reached out and touched her hair and felt himself tremble. He'd wanted to fill his hands with her hair for so long. "It's lovely, Justine. Your hair is like liquid fire. It's as vital and beautiful as you. Yes, beautiful," he repeated.

Justine looked down, concentrating on spreading out the picnic, but he could see that tears had filled her eyes. He wanted to kiss her, to take her in his arms, protect her. He could feel the need growing inside of him. Then she looked up. She'd blinked away the tears, and she was smiling. "Thanks for the compliment. I'll just get back into my clothes, and I'll be ready for lunch."

She slipped through the thick trees at the edge of the jungle, walking a little farther than was necessary to make sure she was out of Logan's sight. She'd worn her bathing suit under her clothes but had remembered to bring underwear with her. Justine dressed quickly and, with her clothes back on, felt more secure. She'd been vulnerable before, even to his words. They'd brought back the past and almost made her cry. She'd be all right now.

They ate the sandwiches prepared by the inn and drank a fruity punch in silence. It wasn't a comfortable silence, Logan thought. There was a tension in it, which was all his fault. In wanting to get to know her, he'd touched on the most sensitive areas. He'd gotten too close. He didn't care. He felt as if he were beginning to know her at last, and the surprise of learning about her insecurities was far outweighed by the tenderness he felt for her because of them. Something of Justine the superstar had lingered in his vision of her and he admitted that he'd remained a little in awe of it. Now it was gone. The woman he felt such tenderness for was here beside him—and there was nothing of the superstar about her.

Logan pushed a little more, somehow convinced that now that he was getting to know her, he couldn't let her slip away. As they finished lunch and packed everything in the basket the inn had supplied, Logan asked, "When you were a child, did someone make you think you weren't pretty?" He knew he was overstepping the very carefully drawn boundaries but he didn't care. It was now or never. She was too close to talking about herself for him to let her step behind them again, even if she refused to answer. At least he would have tried, and he might never have another chance.

"Yes," she said softly. The plates and utensils were packed. Logan moved them aside. "Maybe we should put them in the car," Justine suggested. She looked at her watch, and Logan knew he could lose her now.

He picked up the basket, took her hand and started toward the Jeep. "Would you go for a walk with me first, before we leave?" His hand was still on her arm. "I'd thought we might stay longer, spend the whole day here, in fact," he said, knowing that he was the one forcing her to leave by forcing her to talk about herself. He didn't care. It was time.

"Just for a few minutes," she said, walking ahead of him and causing Logan to wonder if she hadn't accepted just to be able to move away from his touch on her arm. There'd been electricity in the touch. He'd felt it through his fingers and up his arm and into his chest where it had caught and quickened his heartbeat. She'd felt the shock, too. He knew that because he'd seen her tremble. He wasn't alone with the feeling; it was happening to both of them, and he was going to let it happen.

Dammit, he thought to himself, they were attracted to each other. Justine wasn't a child, she'd been married to Brady Hart and, according to what Frank had told him, she'd been hurt. Well, he wasn't going to hurt her. Whatever happened, he'd never hurt her.

They were walking side by side but not touching. "Who told you?" he asked.

"Told me what?"

"That you weren't . . . that you . . ." Logan was hesitant.

"That I was plain? My mother," Justine responded flatly. "She said I'd never go anywhere even if I could sing because I didn't have the looks of a star." Justine shook her head thoughtfully. "And she'd hoped for a star, believe me, so she could get out of there." Justine didn't explain any further, and Logan didn't push.

"She was wrong about my future, though," Justine said finally.

"*And* about everything else," Logan replied. The breeze had come up, and it caught Justine's hair, tossing the curls across her face. His hand reached out and touched one of the curls, brushing it back from her forehead. The gesture was automatic, almost as if he weren't controlling his own hand.

The sky had suddenly clouded over, and at the same time that she felt his touch, Justine felt a raindrop and then another on her face. His touch was as soft as the rain, and she knew that something was happening to her. She'd told him what she'd never told anyone before, admitting that she'd always been unsure about herself, about her looks.

They were standing in the middle of the narrow strip of sand that separated the jungle from the sea, a hundred yards away from the Jeep. Out over the lagoon the sky had turned black and the clouds were growing, coming their way. The rain had begun.

"We better get back to the inn," Justine said.

"Yes." He took her hand as they turned and began to walk, and then to run. By the time they reached the Jeep, the rain was coming down hard. Logan started to open the door and then changed his mind, pulling her toward the lean-to.

"Logan—"

He'd grabbed the towels from the top of the lunch basket. "Come on—let's get under cover until it stops," he called out as they ran. "We'll be drenched if we try to get back to the inn in that Jeep."

They raced for cover, and she was laughing now, as if somehow the rain had released her tension. They dived under the palm fronds that covered the shed, and Logan dropped the towels on the ground. The rain was coming straight down in heavy sheets, but they were completely dry in an area no more than eight by ten feet. Although they could reach out and feel the rain, the thick roof of the structure protected them from even a drop.

"It's so... homey," Justine said suddenly, turning to him with a smile on her face. Far in the distance, thunder roared, and then lightning streaked across the now black sky. Justine jumped slightly, and Logan reached out for her.

"Are you afraid?" he asked.

"No," she answered, and then added in a strong voice that was almost defensive, "Not of lightning. Not of anything like that."

He knew that what she said was true. She probably never had been physically afraid, but still there was a fear in her which he couldn't understand or even describe. Someday, he told himself, he'd be able to identify it. Now he wanted to protect her from that unnamed fear. That's why he took her into his arms, just when she denied being afraid, and just when he knew better.

Justine let herself be held as the rain pounded around them and the thunder roared overhead. This was different from last night when they'd danced together, and she knew that immediately. While she'd felt a sensuality that was exciting then, she'd been able to name it and at last when the evening ended, to step away from it. Now it infused her and thrilled her, and she didn't want to step away. She knew that she wouldn't have moved, even if the rain hadn't been pounding down around them, she would have stayed there in his arms.

He was the one who stepped back but only long enough to look down at her and try to read the expression on her face. His eyes held hers during that long moment. Everything around her disappeared, the pouring rain, the dark sky that turned the lagoon inky black, the scent of flowers heady in the downpour, even the feeling on her skin of the raindrops left over from their run to shelter. Everything disappeared but Logan. He stood over her, looking down at her, his dark hair falling over his forehead, his blue eyes the only blue left in the stormy afternoon. He'd dressed, too, but never bothered to button his shirt. She could see his chest rising and falling with each breath.

Justine had no doubts anymore, and when his hands reached out to cup her face so he could look deeply into her eyes, she leaned toward him, raising her face to his, standing on tiptoe and closing her eyes just as his lips brushed hers lightly for the first time.

Logan felt himself tremble almost violently with that first touch of his lips on hers, and he hesitated, afraid that he was going to lose control and the gentleness that went with that control.

Then he lost it, lost it completely as his mouth came down forcefully on hers and his arms enclosed her against him. But it was all right, it was all right, he told himself as his head spun with the wonder of it all, for she was holding him with the same force.

Her mouth opened under his, and his tongue slid inside with a silky, satiny probing. He heard a moan escape from one or both of them as he moved his hands up and down her back, feeling the heat of her skin beneath the flimsy cotton T-shirt, pulling her even closer until her breasts were crushed against his bare chest.

He kissed her again and again until her mouth was bruised by the kisses. Then he buried his face in her hair and whispered, "Justine, Justine..." He meant to ask her if she wanted him, if she was as ready for him as he thought, but she answered before he even asked.

"Yes," she said. "Yes, Logan." It was an affirmation of her need, a response to his need.

"I want you here, now," he said huskily with his mouth still against her flaming curls. Somehow he managed to move away again and spread the big downy towels out on the hard-packed sand. The wind had picked up and a fine spray of rainwater blew into the shed and dampened his face. He smiled and looked up at her. She was smiling, too, and trembling a little from the wind.

"Well, it's drier here than anywhere else," he said, not even realizing that the words he spoke sounded hoarse, roughened by the emotions that were raging through him. She reached down and touched his dark hair with her fingertips, running them through the fine thick strands. That touch, so familiar and sweet, made his head spin, and when he got up, he did so shakily. "Oh God, Justine, I—"

She was in his arms, not letting him finish the sentence, hungrily seeking his lips with hers, this time letting her tongue work magic, exploring, tasting, loving his mouth while her hands pulled at his open shirt until, with his help, she slipped it off and at last touched the hard bare skin that she'd imagined touching. She'd been right. It *was* like touching a flame; it burned through the palms of her hands and singed her fingertips as she dug them into the hard flesh.

Logan knew from her touch that her need was just as great as his. He drew his mouth away, still holding her, so he could take off her shirt, too. Justine had already anticipated him, and as he watched in wonder she reached down and pulled the shirt over her head. His breath caught when he saw through the bra the outline of her dark nipples, hard and taut. He cupped both breasts in his hands and then with curious excited fingers, pulled down the front of her bra and let her breasts spill out. "Beautiful," he said as he bent down to take one stiff nipple in his mouth.

"Oh, Logan," Justine whispered when she felt his mouth enclose the tender point so hungrily while at the same time his hand found her other breast, teasing and taunting. She cried out again, intoxicated by his hands and lips.

Finally he reached behind her and unhooked the bra, pulling it away and dropping it onto the towel on top of his flowered shirt. They stood together, bare from the waist up, their hands still exploring the territory so new and wonderful to them. They looked and touched until Logan said softly, "I think we should..." He finally stopped his roaming hands. "Slow down for a moment and..."

"Take off the rest of our clothes?" Justine found herself finishing for him.

Logan smiled a smile that was sweeter than she'd ever seen. He was already unzipping his long cotton pants, but he didn't move as quickly as Justine. With one motion she hooked her thumbs in the elastic top of her flimsy shorts and pulled them and the bikini panties beneath them off together, stepped out and left them where she stood.

If he'd been able to pause, he might have laughed, certainly smiled, at her quicksilver motion, but he didn't pause. She was too beautiful. He swept her in his arms and then laid her down on the towels and knelt beside her, looking down in wonder at the soft skin pinkened by the sun except for the two white patches that had been covered by her green bikini. He smiled again. It was a gentle, loving smile and he saw it mirrored on her lips as she looked up at him. Her brown eyes were wide with wonder and desire. Logan felt so proud, so happy, that he'd pleased her until now and would continue to please her, for he knew he would. Nothing but pleasure and sweetness could come from what was about to happen to them.

One of his hands still rested on her slim leg, and he leaned over to taste the inside of her ankle with his lips before working his way up her calf to her thigh and then beyond. He paused, his hands parted her legs and his lips brushed her triangle of red curls.

When he touched her, a coil of desire tightened, curled and twisted through Justine until she thought she would scream. Instead her hands reached out and touched him, letting him know what she wanted with inquisitive, delighted fingers that lingered there as his fingers lingered on her.

But not for long. There was something else, something more, they needed, and they were both ready. Justine opened herself for him as Logan rose above her, and her eyes rested briefly on his broad shoulders and chest, his flat abdomen and the hard arousal that showed his need. She looked, drinking in the beauty of his tanned hard body but only briefly, for he'd leaned over and as his hands nestled in her hair, held her face against his.

Just as their lips touched, she moved her long legs and he knew that she wanted just what he wanted.

She opened her eyes wide to look at him, and his words caught in his throat. All he could think of was having her, taking her now and being inside of her until they were where he'd ached so long for them to be.

Justine arched to meet him, and he slid deep, deep inside until he was lodged there and she tightened around him for an instant. Then he began to move faster, almost leaving her warmth and then plunging deep inside again. She moved with him, clinging tightly, holding on, her eyes locked with his while the lightning flashed, the thunder roared and the rain beat down all around them.

Together they moved in perfect unison, meeting each other thrust for thrust, with longing and then deep satisfaction at this blending of their two bodies, which had never been more ready for each other. Justine felt as though she were a flame amid the storm that would continue to blaze as long as she was here beneath him. Logan was making love to her with passion and power barely checked, along with tenderness. It took her to the limits of her emotions and made her feel that any moment she would break through those bonds and be hurled beyond passion to some other world she'd never known.

Faster and faster he thrust within her until she felt that last semblance of control disappear in the hot passion of their need. Then in a starburst of white-hot ecstasy, she saw the bright flash of that other world.

It was in Logan's eyes. They seemed to catch the light from the skies as everything around them turned into a peaceful glow. It lasted for an eternity, that moment in the blinding white light. Logan saw it as clearly as Justine did. He was caught in it, too, and it flashed through him with the lightning.

Finally they lay exhausted, intertwined on the rumpled towels, and Justine whispered, "Nothing like that has ever..."

"Me, too," he answered softly, and she knew it was the same for him as for her. She smiled as she nestled next to him and listened to the rain that grew softer and softer and finally ended, leaving a rainbow across the lagoon that was made of every color missing from that moment of blazing white they'd experienced together.

Chapter Five

The rainbow had faded in the sky as they walked arm in arm back to the Jeep. The sun had come out and brightened the jungle around them, leaving each blossom, each leaf, shining with the last vestiges of the rain. Raindrops glistened, too, in their hair and on their skin. Like all of nature around them, Logan and Justine seemed to have been freshened and cleansed.

Logan hugged her once lovingly as she stepped up into the Jeep before he went around to his side, got in, started the engine and flashed her a smile. He looked so different, so young, Justine thought, knowing that she looked different, too. She could feel the freshness on her skin, in her eyes and on her lips as she returned his smile. She felt a thrill race through her and warm her with memories of what had just passed between them. Justine knew that it was rare for two people to ignite with such breathtaking force. Rare and wonderful and somehow dangerous. She'd meant to be wary, but it wasn't easy, not with him beside her, watching her.

They'd reached the top of the bumpy hill and turned onto the highway. Keeping part of his attention on the road, he reached over and touched her face. "It's still early. We have the whole night before us." He wasn't thinking of the mail boat; in fact, he'd forgotten it, and so had she.

Justine caught his hand and held it to her face as they drove the rest of the way back to the inn in silence, living in their separate thoughts of each other. Only when she got back to her room and Logan came in behind her and took her in his arms as the door closed did she pause to speak or try to.

His lips stopped her with a kiss and after that a wish. "If only this could go on and on."

Then she spoke the words his lips had silenced, looking up at him with serious eyes. "I never imagined it happening between us like this, so..."

"Perfectly," he said, reaching for another kiss.

While it had been perfect, that wasn't the word Justine searched for. Unexpected, surprising, thrilling, and as she'd thought before, somehow dangerous. That was the most relevant word, dangerous, and not to be repeated. "Logan," she began, pulling away a little from his firm and possessive hold. "Logan, we have to talk about this."

He smothered her lips again with his. "No, we don't, not now. What we have to do is eat and drink and celebrate what's happened between us. What we have to do is...go dancing!" He laughed. "I feel like dancing with you again. And after that..." He smiled a sexily sweet smile that almost melted her.

Almost, but not quite. "Logan—"

She couldn't win. "Nope, no talking about anything except our dancing plans for tonight." He dropped another light and sweet kiss on her lips, lifting his eyebrows and murmuring, "Hmm," and kissing her again more thoroughly. "Yes, I remember that," he whispered as he started to deepen the kiss.

Justine was resolved this time, so she stepped completely away from him.

"All right, all right," he said, throwing up his hands. "No more. Get yourself dressed, and I'll be back in time to take you to dinner and dancing. After that we can talk," he said, relenting.

Logan knew why he'd avoided that "talk" she was so insistent about. She was planning to remind him of their totally separate lives, their very different careers, their business association that should remain just that, business. He knew what was on her mind, but he also knew none of it mattered for two people who felt as they'd felt during their afternoon on the beach. Perfect was the right word. He'd never known anything like what had happened between them, and he remembered—he would never forget—her words. Nothing like it had ever happened for her, either. She'd said that to him afterward, and he'd believed her. That made all the difference, Logan decided as he went into his room, whistling. Yes, he thought, this was certainly different. He hadn't whistled in years.

Justine heard the whistle, for she was still standing at the door of her room trying hard to collect her thoughts, to gather her wits, which had definitely fled.

Finally she forced herself to leave the spot where she'd been glued. She'd decided on a long bath, so she could sort out her thoughts. They were going in all directions and needed to be called back.

Justine filled the tub, took off the clothes that she'd been in and out of a number of times during the day and stepped into the cool water. She knew perfectly well what was happening to her. The compartmentalizing of her life that she'd been so proud of in the past two years had run amok. The compartments were empty. Everything was a confusion of thoughts and hopes and dreams, none of which were realistic or even possible.

Yet she couldn't help remembering Logan's kisses, his long hard body covering hers, their time together at the edge of the jungle as the rain pounded down around them. So beautiful, so... What had Logan said? Perfect. A perfect romance, but a romance that was one part tropical island, one part fantasy and the rest serendipity. It wouldn't, couldn't last.

In fact, Justine realized as she turned off the faucets and let the soapy water wash over her, it would all be over very soon. While they'd been gone, the boat that they'd both forgotten had surely arrived and by now the radio was probably repaired.

They *had* forgotten about it, she realized. But fortunately Justine remembered. There was still plenty of daylight left. If they radioed the charter company for help, a plane could get to them before dark. She pulled out the plug in the tub, stood up and reached for a towel. They needed to send a message now, right away.

Wearing a yellow sundress she'd bought in the village but with her hair still hanging in wet curls to her shoulders, Justine knocked on Logan's door. He answered quickly, expectantly, and she allowed herself a precious moment to look at him. He'd shaved and there was a glow of tan on his face. He was wearing a deep purple polo shirt that made his eyes look almost black. Justine opened her mouth to tease him about buying so many clothes when she remembered why she was there.

"The boat," she blurted out. "The boat must have come by now, Logan. If we hurry we can get a message off so there'll still be enough light—"

He was shaking his head and smiling. Reaching out, he grabbed her arm and pulled her into the room. "You look gorgeous in that sundress," he said, kissing her decisively. "Just gorgeous."

"Logan—"

"The mail boat didn't come," he whispered against her ear, as if murmuring words of love.

Startled, Justine looked up at him. "I thought Martin said today at the latest." This wasn't working, Justine decided. Her plan was going completely awry.

Logan shook his head. "Remember the storm?" His smile was lovable. "I hope you do. I remember it very well." He managed to steal another kiss. "Well, the consensus is that the boat got caught in bad weather."

"What consensus?" Justine was still a little skeptical.

"The one taken downstairs among the folks who are in the know and who're slightly less vague than our friend Martin. Seems that whenever there's a threat of storm, the mail boat ties up in a safe harbor and waits. Could be a couple more days because, apparently, this storm hit our area first. Now it's moving north toward other islands in the chain. So," he said with a wicked smile, "what about dinner and dancing?"

So much for my compartments, Justine thought as she smiled her affirmative answer.

They had dinner just as the night before, in the restaurant at the inn, but tonight was much different. There was no wedding party, no crush of people celebrating. The other difference was with Justine and Logan. The last time they'd been on edge, wary, unsure of what would transpire between them. Tonight was easy. During the intervening day they'd become friends and become lovers. Since the news of the mail boat, Justine had decided to relax and give herself to the fantasy they were living. It was for now, and they'd think about the rest when it happened.

Steve and Angelique were also at the inn. Apparently Frangipani boasted the only restaurant on the island except for the fruit and seafood stands up on the hill, and everyone who dined out came here.

"Guess you heard the news?" Steve asked as he paused at their table with Angelique, who was wearing a dress of lacy blue cotton, perhaps a gift from the attentive pilot.

Logan grinned. "Yes, it's a shame about the mail boat."

"A terrible shame," Steve agreed, directing Angelique toward a table secluded in one corner of the room.

"The lovers head for the corners," Logan said to Justine with a smile. "Just like us." Indeed, they were also hidden away, even more privately because of a huge tropical plant that blocked them from the view of the other tables.

"It's certainly not the place from which to see and be seen," Justine said.

"Except for the one table directly behind us. Don't turn around now, but someone is watching you."

Justine adjusted her chair slightly so that she could glance in the direction Logan indicated without seeming obvious. "Wonder what such a distinguished-looking man is doing here?" Justine asked, eager to speculate.

"He's probably a wealthy European businessman on vacation," Logan guessed.

"Here alone?"

"Sure. He just made a deal on one of the other islands—maybe La Quinta—and came over for a little peace and quiet."

"How'd he get here?" Justine queried.

"By boat, just like the other tourists."

"Today? You've forgotten about the storm."

"True." Logan glanced over at the next table and could see that their neighbor was quite distinguished, above middle age with gray hair and a short-cropped beard. He was smoking a thin black cigar, and the smoke curled up around him as he sipped a glass of wine.

"Who do you suppose he is?" Justine asked, intrigued.

"I don't know. We'll just have to make up a life for him," Logan suggested.

Throughout their meal they devised various possibilities and finally decided that he was a German automobile manufacturer with a wife and four grown sons, none of them adequately equipped to take over their father's company.

"His wife drinks," Justine decided over dessert and coffee.

"Yes, they've been considering a divorce but are having problems with the property division."

"Do you suppose he has a girlfriend?" Justine wondered.

"I believe, in his case, we would call her his mistress," Logan corrected. "Her name is Brunhilde."

"Oh, no." Justine laughed. "She's more sophisticated. Marlene, I think."

When they looked over again, the object of their conjectures had finished dinner and left the restaurant. "Now, we'll never know," Justine said sadly.

"It's better that way," Logan assured her with mock seriousness. They were enjoying themselves, he thought with pleasure. An unexpected sense of fun had enveloped them. He'd never been more content, more at ease with a woman in his life. He looked at her and smiled, wanting to hold her again while the memory of her lovely body beneath his was so fresh.

"Now for the dancing," Logan said as they finished their coffee and he signed the check.

"To the tune of the jukebox again?" she asked.

"I don't think we have much choice since the band didn't show up tonight."

They drifted into the little café only to find that others had preceded them. The room was crowded, and many of the couples were dancing. "We won't be alone on the floor tonight," Logan observed, "but I'm not going to notice the others," he added, sliding his hand around to the small of her back. "What about you?"

She fit into his arms, resting her head just below his chin and snuggling close as they moved gently to the music. "There's no one here but us," Justine answered dreamily.

As far as the two of them were concerned, she was right. They danced that way, easily, without letting the room into their reverie. There was only Justine and Logan, only the moment, and with each song that played, they found the beat and swayed to it.

Then Logan saw their mystery man from the restaurant. He was sitting alone again, at a table by the bar, smoking his narrow black cigar. "Well, well," Logan whispered in her ear, "guess who's here?" He turned Justine around so that she had a direct view.

Justine looked over Logan's shoulder but without much enthusiasm this time. "I can't seem to concentrate on his story," she whispered as she moved closer, fitting perfectly into Logan's long body just as one of her songs began to play on the jukebox.

"Sing it for me," Logan said, and she did, softly.

"No, come on, really sing it. You've never sung for me before."

"I'm not going to now, either," she vowed. "Not here with all these people around."

"Why not?" he egged her on. "You'll never see them again. I thought performers loved to do their thing in public. Come on, Justine, sing."

She let him talk her into it, opening up her voice a little more. Those closest to them on the dance floor paused to listen. Then a few others stopped dancing, and soon the whole room was silently attentive, listening to the voice they all recognized. When the record ended, Justine began the refrain again, her voice stronger as she gave herself to the song. It was one of her favorites, a rock ballad, "Our Song Unending." She'd written it herself, at the height of her career when she'd finally gained the confidence to put her own words to music. It was a pure, simple lyric that she'd always believed in.

As the song came to an end, Logan saw their mysterious admirer stand up at his table, and as he stood he began to clap. He was joined by the rest of the crowd in the room. Justine acknowledged him and the others with a smile and a slight bow before turning back to Logan and whispering, "I have a sudden desire to sing it again."

"Then do it," Logan insisted.

"But just for you." She looked up at him, and he read the look perfectly, seeing in her eyes a desire that he'd last seen there in a little lean-to on the lagoon. It made him weak with need; it was all Logan could do to take her hand and lead her through the room to the lobby, barely noticing that the man who'd instigated the ovation had started to move toward them, seen the look in their eyes and changed his mind.

She sang the song once more, in his room cuddled next to Logan in bed.

I see the writing on the wall
That clearly tells me not to fall.
I don't give it a glance
For this romance means everything to me . . .

Logan held her closer, kissing her throat where the notes, so true and sweet, vibrated. She wrapped her arms around him, and for that moment, breathing his breath as he kissed her gently on the corner of her lips, she believed the words. His arms held her tightly, molding her body to his. The last notes came so softly that he had to put his ear next to her lips to hear them.

A song forever sung
No need for applause
Because . . .

Logan touched her face and looked deeply into her eyes, knowing this was a song that had been written long ago but letting himself believe that because they were together, here, now, it was a song just for them.

My applause
Is my tomorrow
With you . . .

They awoke together at dawn, wrapped in each other's arms. Justine turned slightly, rearranged herself and closed her eyes again. She could feel Logan's breath on the back of her neck, his arm resting on her hip, one of his legs flung over hers. Everywhere, they were touching. The small of her back fit against his abdomen, her shoulders rested on his chest, and one of his hands cupped her breasts familiarly. For now, for today and perhaps tomorrow, for the time left after the storm, she was where she wanted to be, comfortable, and at peace. Beyond that peace, there was still the excitement of being with Logan. Justine sighed audibly and, with those happy thoughts, drifted to sleep. When she awoke again, he was standing beside the bed with a breakfast tray.

"Here or on the patio?" he asked.

"Here," Justine decided lazily. "I don't want to get up yet. What's this?" There was an envelope on the tray.

"Have a look."

She opened it and took out a sheet of thin blue stationery, engraved with the initials "C.G." She looked up at Logan with a frown.

"Carter Graham," he said. "The owner of the airstrip, not to mention that vast mansion in the jungle, which you and Steve were so taken with."

"What in the world?" Justine glanced at the letter quickly and then began to laugh. "I don't believe it! Carter Graham is our friend from last night."

"Yes, the German industrialist with a plump wife and four wastrel sons is an Englishman in the jungle with no family whatsoever, apparently."

"Carter Graham, I know his name." Justine closed her eyes in concentration and then opened them wide with a burst of insight. "Of course, the playwright. Light comedy, farce, that kind of thing. He did quite well a few decades ago. There were even some wonderful British films made from his plays. Nothing heavy, but witty and charming. 'Monsieur Graham' is Carter Graham. Imagine."

"Imagine," Logan teased, "that he recognized you last night even if you didn't know who he was. Seems he's a big fan."

"He wants us to have lunch with him at Savoy's Revenge. Savoy's Revenge," she repeated. "That's the name of the house?"

"I guess so. What do you think?"

"I think it's a weird name."

"No, Justine," he said with a laugh as she managed to unfold herself enough to reach for the cup of coffee he offered. "What do you think about lunch?"

"Sounds marvelous," she said before adding, "as long as we don't have to walk."

"Read on. He's sending a car."

The car was an old Rolls complete with liveried chauffeur. "A definite improvement over our earlier trek through the jungle," Logan decided as they settled back in the leather seats of the silver-gray car. It managed the bumpy road with a sort of Rolls-Royce detachment and arrogance, depositing them by the portico within the huge stone gates of Savoy's Revenge, where Carter Graham stood waiting.

He was wearing a pair of fawn-colored slacks, a pale blue shirt and a navy blue ascot with white polka dots. As before, he was smoking a narrow black cigar, looking like a character from one of his plays. "From Cuba," he informed them casually. "I still have some connections there. One should never burn all of one's bridges. That's my motto. Welcome to Savoy's Revenge." He took Justine's hand in his firm grasp and brought it to his lips. "Miss Hart. I've long been a fan of yours so you can imagine my pleasure in finding you at the inn. I recognized you before you sang, of course. Being such an admirer, I was naturally charmed by your rendition of that lovely song."

He turned to acknowledge Logan. "Of course, I'm familiar with your firm, Mr. Addison. I also know your father's, and understand you're giving him some fierce competition in your business. Good for you. I favor youthful endeavors above all else," he said with a twinkle in his eye.

Luncheon was served in the smaller of two dining rooms, which was furnished like the rest of the house in an eclectic, out-of-the-jungle style. "We used as many native products as possible, but of course many of the furnishings had to be brought in from the States, including building materials for the house itself. It was five years being built. Supplies reached here step by step from Miami to the larger islands and on to St. Cat's by barge, and labor wasn't easy, either, this island being less than productive in that department. Quite a chore to put it mildly, but worth it."

"It's a lovely house," Justine agreed, charmed by the house and by her host.

"It's my revenge on the Savoy Hotel, where I lived for many years in that damnable English weather," he said, clarifying the name for them. "Now, let me hear all about you, what brings you to my island?" It *was* his island, they learned later, for Carter owned most of it, including the landing strip built for his private use, thereby prohibiting a large tourist trade from invading his sanctuary.

"We had engine trouble," Justine explained.

"Obviously," came the amused reply. "I was told about the two men and a woman who managed to find my field just at twilight. I flew in the next day. Of course, I had no idea who my guests were until I ventured to town," he said to Logan. "Now, what brought you to the Caribbean?"

They were having the first course, a conch soup that was even better than the hotel's, served with a chilled white wine. Justine was too delighted by the tastes of the exquisite soup to answer so Logan explained their venture to La Quinta.

"Ah, yes," Carter said. "I've had a look at the club there myself. Your firm is involved in the financing?" he asked Logan, who nodded. "And you, my dear," he said, addressing Justine. "What is your decision about La Quinta?"

"Affirmative," she said between spoonfuls of soup.

"Good," came the response. "I will invest as well. Perhaps we can discuss it later, Logan?" He waited for Logan's assent before announcing, "Now, for the next course."

They made their way through that course and the one after while Carter regaled them with stories of the building of Savoy's Revenge. "Actually it was a dream of my wife's and mine to have a retreat, far from the cold. But each time we made plans something came up, another play or a revival or a movie and so our plans got pushed further and further away. Then my wife died, and for ten years I became a nomad. I've lived in the best hotels in the world from Raffles in Singapore to the Gritti Palace in Venice but it became cumbersome after a while, traveling with all that baggage. I need my belongings around me to feel comfortable," he explained. "Finally I decided to build the house that Anne and I had fantasized about. I just wish she had lived to see it."

Then with a determined smile that told them more than words that he thought about his wife and often, Carter continued. "This house gives me a place to hide away in when I'm tired of traveling, and speaking of traveling," he said as dessert and champagne were served, "I understand you have been trying for several days to get back to the States. Alas, we've had a weather problem that prevented Martin from repairing his radio." Carter smiled at their astonished looks. "Ah, yes. I know everything that happens here on St. Cat's. In any case, we don't need to wait for Martin. I will radio ahead for you, and you can be flown to Miami on my plane. Tonight, if you wish. Or tomorrow..."

"Tomorrow," Logan and Justine said in unison, eliciting a knowing smile from Carter.

"Just so. But you *will* return, next time as my guests."

* * *

"Something tells me we would never be successful fortune-tellers," Logan said when they arrived back at the hotel.

Justine laughed. "We certainly missed on Carter, but of course that plant was in the way..."

"No excuse," Logan decided. "We didn't even have his nationality right, and no one looks more British than Carter. Are we going to accept his invitation to return to St. Cat's as his houseguests?"

Justine didn't answer, and Logan decided not to pursue the subject, not immediately, anyway. Now, in midafternoon, they had no desire for dinner and no energy for a swim. "Let's just laze around in my room," Logan suggested. "How does that sound?"

"Lovely," Justine responded, trying not to think about the morning when, at last, they would be leaving their island paradise.

At around nine o'clock, following a late afternoon of lovemaking that was, if possible, more satisfying than ever, they give in to hunger pangs and ordered sandwiches from the café.

"I never thought I'd be able to eat again after that five-course lunch," Justine said, taking a huge bite of her club sandwich. Ensconced in Logan's bed, she was wearing his St. Cat's T-shirt and nothing else. Logan had pulled on a pair of cotton shorts, and his hair was uncombed, falling over his tanned forehead. Justine reached out and brushed it back with a loving hand. "You look so different without your glasses. You haven't worn them since we landed on Carter's airstrip," she observed.

"I'd like to say they're only for reading, but I must admit I can see a lot better with them on," he confided, taking a sip from his glass of rum punch. "You haven't even had on the ubiquitous red sunglasses in a couple of days."

"I know. At first I felt naked without them, but they didn't really fit our adventure, either. On La Quinta, yes, but not on St. Cat's."

"About La Quinta, Justine. I want you to be sure before making any decisions."

"Are you saying it's not a good deal?" she questioned.

"No, it's a good deal. Carter's interest is further proof of that, but I don't want to let what's happened between us—"

"Don't worry, Logan," she interrupted with a smile. "I'm too good a businesswoman to be swayed by a personal relationship. I learned that long ago." She paused to consume the rest of her sandwich, and Logan waited patiently for her to tell him about what happened in that "long ago" to change her. She didn't comply, and once more he let the subject drop, determined to pick it up again before the night ended.

"No," she said, wiping her mouth with a linen napkin, "my decision is based on the merits of the proposition and my belief in you and Frank. I want to go with La Quinta."

"I'm pleased. It's a good decision that you won't regret." Logan put their plates on the bedside table and handed Justine her tall glass of punch. "I guess we won't be drinking this again for a while," he said rather sadly before returning to the subject. "In our business dealings, La Quinta and the rest, I want to assure you, Justine, that I won't combine that with our personal..." he struggled to explain, "relationship, and what's happened between us."

She looked at him seriously, and although her red sunglasses were nowhere to be seen, he felt as though she'd put them back on. "You promised me that we could talk, Logan, and we never have. I think it's time."

Logan leaned back against the headboard and waited.

"This has all been idyllic and perfect, but it's fantasy. I'm sure you see that, too," she said.

He didn't answer.

"You *do* see it, Logan? None of this would have happened in New York. It wouldn't even have happened on La Quinta. There's something about St. Cat's..."

"Or something about us when we're on St. Cat's," he completed. "Maybe here we become ourselves, our *real* selves."

"No, here we become what we can never be in New York. We each have our own roles back there. They're our true roles, Logan."

"The lines can't be crossed?" He was determined to push her, make her answer in specifics.

"They *shouldn't* be crossed. It's not wise to mix business and personal lives. I know that better than anyone," she added almost bitterly. "I tried it."

Logan thought carefully before he responded. "I'm not Brady, Justine. I don't want to be judged beside him." Logan was calmly defensive.

"I know," she said, "but I also know the consequences of mixing business with personal lives, no matter who's involved. It's difficult to explain, and you'd have trouble understanding."

"Try me, Justine."

"It's still so painful. It still hurts, and I never want to go through anything like it again."

He put his hand on her arm. It wasn't a sexual touch but a reassuring, comforting one.

"I was so poor, Logan, poorer than any of the islanders here or on La Quinta. My father was a sharecropper. My mother worked downtown in the dime store, and she hated every minute of it. She spent her life wanting out, and for a while, when I was a child, she thought she could get out vicariously through me. But she was too bitter even to give that hope a chance and could only put me down, knowing it would never happen. Sometimes I wish she could have lived to see how it all turned out. Honestly, I don't know whether I wish that because I'd like to think of her being happy for me or whether I'd like to have been able to prove she was wrong. Because she did hurt me, Logan."

He held her close, happy to hear her talk at last, sad to know the truth of her life.

"I had nothing but my dreams and my talent, and I couldn't be sure they were enough—especially with my mother's negative attitude. Then Brady Hart came along with his band. It was in the early, very formative stages, but they were getting close to a good sound. Brady said I could be their best instrument, the voice to complete their sound. I started singing with them. It happened so fast, so big, that no one could believe it, least of all Brady and me. But it was true. He'd created a sound. He'd also created a star in Justine."

She looked out into space, not focusing on anything, remembering. "He took me out of poverty, gave me my career. I loved him, and he became my whole life. Then he took it all away."

"Not you, Justine. You were still there, and you were a real talent," Logan reminded her.

"He *nearly* took it all," she insisted. "At first there was very little left of me. I remember thinking so often that if I couldn't trust Brady, my lover, my partner..." There were tears in her eyes, anguish in her voice.

Logan was silent for a long time as he tried to get into her mind, tried to understand her feelings. "Trust has to be earned over years and years, Justine. It's not instant. Fame happened to you instantly, and you let trust go along with it. I'm not asking for instant anything. Not for instant trust or love or even instant friendship. I'm asking for a chance. I want us to try it together when we get home and see what happens."

Justine shook her head. "This fantasy we have isn't real, Logan. It can't last. It's as fragile as those raindrops that blew into the shed yesterday and then disappeared. At the first stress, the first sign of strain, we'd fall apart."

"You're predestining us to failure, Justine. That's not the way it has to be." He reached out then and grabbed her, almost roughly, pulling her toward him and kissing her. Lost in the kiss, Justine found herself melting again, melting into him with the same feelings of need and desire that she'd been overcome by since the afternoon at the lagoon, or even before, since that first night on the balcony. She returned his kiss hungrily. Then she pulled away, or tried to. "It won't work. We're so different, our lives—"

"Give it a chance, Justine. It could be wonderful."

She felt herself surrendering to his words and to *him*, the Logan she'd discovered so completely on St. Cat's. "I'm not sure—"

"Neither am I," he said with a laugh, "not sure of anything except the way I feel about you. Feelings count for something, Justine. Let's give it a try. We'll slip back into the States, fly to New York and then pick up where we left off. If you'd like, we'll keep it a secret. No one will have to know, not even Frank. Will that make you feel better?"

Justine looked at him, thinking that in spite of his vast knowledge and intellect, Logan was very naive. He didn't realize what life around Justine Hart would be like. She touched his face, almost sadly. "I wish I could believe."

Logan held her close. "We're leaving early tomorrow, and I don't want to spend any more of our time together talking about what might be. This is our last night here. What I want isn't fantasy. I want you, Justine. Now and for the rest of the night." He kissed her again, his hands buried in her hair, pressing her lips to his, drinking deeply as, like two rivers of energy, they flowed toward each other and converged.

Chapter Six

This way," a voice called out.

Logan looked over the heads of the crowd as he and Justine stepped from the plane into the heavy Miami air. A tall, thin young man in a blue airport blazer was coming toward them. Logan's first thought was that the kid would never make it. Then a phalanx of police appeared and began to push through the crowd of reporters, photographers and fans. The airport attendant kept coming, weaving in and out, one hand high above his head, clutching his walkie-talkie from which a disembodied voice issued garbled instructions. Logan could only hope that the man—and the police—reached them before he and Justine disappeared into the stampeding mob.

"Did you know it was going to be like this?" he shouted to her as they watched the human wave wash toward them.

"Yes," she cried out, "but if I'd told you, you wouldn't have believed me."

"True," Logan said. That ended their conversation. The photographers had closed in.

"Justine!" half a dozen voices shouted, "this way." She complied, turning first one way and then another, flashing a smile, her red sunglasses now firmly back in place. Reporters' voices joined in, staccato fashion, coming at them like gunfire.

"What happened on St. Cat's, Justine?"

"Is that the guy—Addison?"

"Turn this way, Addison."

"Is it true that you planned this whole thing to get away together?"

"Was it all a publicity stunt, Justine?"

"Did you want us to think you were dead?"

"Justine, this way. Addison, put your arm around her, how about it?"

Logan did hold her close, not for the reporters but to keep her from being separated from him by the mob.

Finally a wide swath opened up with police holding back the fans on each side. "Follow me," the attendant said. "The VIP lounge is just ahead. We'll make it," he added with what confidence he could muster.

Logan had the odd sensation that they weren't walking at all but were being carried through the crowd as it closed behind them and began to push. He'd never experienced anything quite like the noise and the crush or the cameras and the questions flung at them.

They could see a door ahead. It opened slightly and then, just as they reached it, was flung wide and seemed to swallow them up. They were digested by a narrow hall and then spilled out into a big room where everything was suddenly calm and quiet.

"Well, thank God." A tall middle-aged woman sitting on one of the VIP chairs got up and came toward them. "I wasn't about to go out into that mob to greet you. This young man was good enough to bring you to me." She turned toward the attendant who'd been flung into the lounge with them, shook his hand and requested, "Now, I think we all need something refreshing to drink." That done, she greeted Justine with outstretched arms. "Glad to welcome you back into the land of the living, darling."

Justine returned the hug before introducing Logan. "This is Logan Addison, my partner in the little adventure," she said. "Logan, Adele Schwartz, my manager and my close friend."

"Well," Adele said, pumping Logan's hand enthusiastically, "what did you think about your greeting out there, your welcome to the U.S.A.?"

"Compared to that, the plane crash was nothing. They're like vultures," he said.

"Ah, here're our drinks. You two need this more than I, but I feel a little rumpled myself, vicariously, by your experience. So—" she clinked her glass against each of theirs "—to the resurrection of Justine Hart and Logan... Dear Lord, I do believe I've forgotten your last name!"

"Addison," Justine informed her, adding to Logan, "She's very vague about things. Not at all like your typical manager."

"Which is why you adore me so," Adele finished for her. "I must say, Justine, this little adventure of yours has been good for business. There was a mad rush to buy up all your old records. I believe the collectors must have decided that if you were dead, they'd better store up on original releases. It was quite incredible. I didn't worry, of course," Adele added. "My guru told me you were okay, so I've been having a marvelous time."

Justine laughed. "And all the while I was sure that you and Frank would be worried to death."

"No, I don't think he was worried, either. I talked to him a couple of times, and he seemed convinced that you two were just off having a little fun. By the look of your gorgeous tans, he was right. The press, of course, had a field day with your obituaries. I saved them all for you, Justine."

They'd settled down on a large comfortable sofa in the middle of the lounge. In other areas, VIP groups had formed to wait for their planes, all of them feigning disinterest in Justine and the hubbub that had accompanied her entrance into the room.

"The rich don't ask for autographs, thank heavens," Adele said. "Anyway, it's all been rather exciting, to tell the truth. Justine's life story was spread across the front pages of the papers. Yours, I'm afraid," she apologized to Logan, "was relegated to page forty-seven or so of the *Times*. You did slightly better in the tabloids."

Logan laughed and began to relax. "That's probably just as well. I don't think my business would be as positively affected by publicity as Justine's."

"I'm really sorry you had to make the news at all, Logan," Justine said. "I expect your father will think

it's all very..." She searched for the right word,
"Tacky."

Logan laughed again. "I'm not with his firm, so it
can't affect him at all, darling. As for Frank, he eats
this kind of thing up. I'm sure he'll be pleased by the
publicity even if it was on page forty-seven."

Logan noticed that his use of the word *darling* had
caused a slight lifting of Adele's eyebrows, nothing
more. He'd slipped in the affectionate term on purpose, just to let Adele know that he and Justine were,
indeed, more than friends and that he planned to remain in the picture.

Justine was pensive. "Actually, I'm concerned that
my past had to be dragged up again. You'd think
they'd had enough of all that."

"Never, my dear," Adele reminded her, "but once
they exhausted the past, they got right into the here
and now—with you two. When they found out that
you were still alive and had been ensconced on a tropical island paradise for three days, well, you can imagine their reaction. Your face is on page one today,
Logan, right up there beside Justine's. The duo of the
year."

"Or more likely of the minute," Justine declared.

Adele laughed a throaty laugh, took a long swallow of her drink and lit a cigarette. "Actually, they
gave you three months as a couple, based on the as-
sumption that Justine is much too worldly for—I'll try
to paraphrase—'the stuffy scion of a well-to-do family.'"

Logan and Justine both burst into laughter, and
when Justine finally caught her breath, she tried to be

comforting, "Oh, Logan, I *am* sorry," but the laugh-ter provided the real apology.

Adele let them enjoy themselves a little longer and then reminded Logan, "Next week—tomorrow, even—a new story will break and you'll be forgotten. For now, however, you two are going to be hounded. I think we better make our plans." She glanced at her watch. "I knew you'd be anxious to get back to work, Logan, and Justine's scheduled for a TV special. They're taping in three days. You cut it close, honey," she told Justine. "I've booked you out on separate planes." She waited for their reaction, which was im-mediate, and then reminded them, "It's the only way. Otherwise, there'll be another mob scene at the gate."

"You're right," Logan agreed. "I'm a novice at this. Just glad you're here to rescue us."

"Well, I had a feeling help would be needed when I got word from the charter company that you were safe and heading home. Someone was bound to have leaked the news to the press, I figured. And was I ever right!" She laughed her throaty laugh. "Especially after the big search."

"Search?" Justine and Logan spoke in unison.

"Oh, yes, the coast guard was out, along with pri-vate planes, most of them curiosity seekers, I expect. Anyway, the word was that the Bermuda Triangle had probably swallowed you up!"

Justine laughed and then exchanged a look with Logan that both of them interpreted correctly. It was a secret wish that the triangle *had* folded them into its welcoming arms and kept them there in some myste-rious paradise. But they were back, back to real life, and it was time to catch their separate planes.

Adele gave Logan his ticket. "You leave first; Justine and I will be on the next nonstop flight to New York an hour later." She glanced at her watch again. "Your flight should be boarding soon. Come on, I'll show you the back way out. You'll be able to slip through the corridor and walk to your gate without being recognized since Justine won't be with you."

"Worst luck," Logan said, smiling down at Justine. "When it's time for you to leave," he said to Adele, seriously, "they're going to recognize Justine. I don't want her to have to go through all that again."

"It's all right, Logan," Justine assured him. "I'm used to it."

"Besides," Adele added, "we have another hour. Some of them will give up and go after another story. We'll also have the police guard. Now you'd better get a move on, Logan."

Logan wouldn't be hurried. "I need a few minutes with Justine," he said with a glance at Adele that caused her to shake her head and collapse down on the blue sofa to wait, lighting another cigarette and picking up a magazine.

Disregarding Adele and everyone else in the room, Logan took Justine in his arms and kissed her lightly.

"We should have said goodbye on the island," she whispered.

"This isn't goodbye, Justine," he insisted, "we're going to see each other again, soon and often."

"You just had a taste of what it's like, Logan. It's crazy."

"It'll die down just like Adele said." His lips touched her cheek sweetly.

"Yes, it'll die down, but not out. Everywhere I go, there's a crowd, maybe not as bad as this one, but it's not the kind of thing you're used to. It can get very irritating very quickly unless—"

"I know, unless you're a star. *Or* unless you want something badly enough. I want you, Justine; I'll deal with the crowds."

She held on to him tightly and could almost believe in the confidence of the man she'd grown to admire on St. Cat's. Yet she felt the need to warn him, at least of what lay immediately ahead. "I'll be rehearsing almost constantly for the next few days since I'm so late."

"Fine. I'll come to the rehearsals."

"No, Logan, you can't. They won't let anyone—"

"All right. I'll pick you up afterward."

Again Justine felt the need to let him know it wasn't going to be that easy. She touched his cheek, trying to soften the hard facts. "They send a car, Logan, and I never know ahead of time when I'll be finished."

"Fine," he said again. "I'll wait. And I'll send the car away. It'll work, Justine. Don't make it complicated." He kissed her again, not so lightly this time, perfectly aware that Adele had put down her magazine and was fidgeting.

"I'm going, Adele," he called to her finally, "and I'll see you both in New York. Depend on it." He kissed Justine one more time to punctuate the seriousness of his decision. Then he turned and walked away, going through a back door, looking down a nearly empty corridor and turning to call out, "Well, my moment of instant fame is over."

The door closed behind him.

IT'S A JACKPOT
OF A GREAT OFFER!

- 4 exciting Silhouette Special Edition novels—FREE!
- a folding umbrella—FREE!
- a surprise mystery bonus that will delight you—FREE!

Silhouette Folding Umbrella— ABSOLUTELY FREE

You'll love your Silhouette umbrella. Its bright color will cheer you up on even the gloomiest day. It's made of rugged nylon to last for years, and is so compact (folds to 15") you can carry it in your purse or briefcase. This folding umbrella is yours free with this offer.

But wait . . . there's even more!

Money-Saving Home Delivery!

Subscribe to Silhouette Special Edition and enjoy the convenience of previewing new, hot-off-the-press books every month, delivered right to your home. Each book is yours for only $1.95—55¢ less per book than what you pay in stores! And there's no extra charge for postage and handling.

Special Extras—Free!

You'll also get our free monthly newsletter—the indispensable insider's look at our most popular writers and their upcoming novels. Now you can have a behind-the-scenes look at the fascinating world of Silhouette. It's an added bonus you'll look forward to every month. You'll also get additional free gifts from time to time as a token of our appreciation for being a home subscriber.

**TAKE A CHANCE ON ROMANCE—
COMPLETE AND MAIL YOUR SCORECARD
TO CLAIM YOUR FREE HEARTWARMING GIFTS**

If offer card below is missing, write to:
Silhouette Books, 120 Brighton Road,
P.O. Box 5084, Clifton, NJ 07015-9956

PLAYER'S SCORECARD

MAIL TODAY

4 FREE BOOKS
FREE FOLDING UMBRELLA

DETACH AND MAIL CARD TODAY

Did you win a
mystery gift?

Place sticker here

Yes! I hit the jackpot. I have affixed my 3 hearts. Please send my 4
Silhouette Special Edition novels free, plus my free folding umbrella
and free mystery gift. Then send me 6 books every month as they
come off the press, and bill me just $1.95 per book—55¢ less than
retail, with no extra charges for postage and handling.

If I am not completely satisfied, I may return a shipment and cancel
at any time. The free books, folding umbrella and mystery gift
remain mine to keep.

CJS 037

NAME _____

ADDRESS _____

APT. _____

CITY_____

STATE _____

ZIP CODE_____

SILHOUETTE "NO-RISK" GUARANTEE
• There is no obligation to buy—the free books and gifts remain yours to keep.
• You pay the lowest price possible—and receive books before they're
available in stores.
• You may end your subscription anytime—just let us know.
Terms and prices subject to change. Offer limited to
one per household and not valid for
present subscribers.

PRINTED IN U.S.A.

Mail this card today for
4 FREE BOOKS
this folding umbrella and
a mystery gift ALL FREE!

* * *

"Well, well." Frank Norwood stood in the doorway of Logan's office, looking past the pile of messages, stacks of documents and papers overflowing the desk to the man behind it. "The prodigal returns. Good to see you, old man."

"I'm glad to be back, I suppose." Logan glanced ruefully at the disarray on his desk. "Half the Western world called and left messages, and there's a portfolio of work to get through on the other half."

"You can ignore the calls that are directly related to your sudden fame." Frank sank into a chair and grinned. "'Mild-mannered financier in love tryst with fiery entertainer.' The newspapers are full of you."

"I've noticed," Logan responded dryly, "although I do believe you've exaggerated the headlines somewhat."

Frank heaved his feet up onto Logan's desk. "Well, they were words to that effect. Anyway, fame is fleeting, and yours is about to come to an end. A Hollywood pair has taken your place by virtue of their billion-dollar divorce settlement and accompanying verbal battles."

"Their misfortune is my gain, I hope." Logan shuffled through the pink telephone slips. "I can also ignore all the messages from my family. How often did my parents call?"

"Your father, only once a day. Now your mother, that's another matter. Three to five times a day at least. We knew less than anyone so you can imagine how often she got in touch with the charter company and with Adele Schwartz. I do hope you've cleared up everything for your parents by now."

"I've checked in with them," was Logan's response. "I suppose I'll have to go up there in the flesh to reassure them that the voice they heard was really mine and to give them the entire story."

"Now, that's just what I want. The entire story," Frank said with lifted eyebrows. "You and captivating Justine. I assume she did captivate you."

"She's a very interesting and intelligent woman," Logan dodged. "By the way," he added, to further distract Frank, "she wants to sign on for La Quinta."

Frank smiled broadly. "So your charms really did work on her. I must admit, I wasn't completely sure."

Logan shook his head. "It was her decision and hers alone, Frank. No one makes up Justine's mind but Justine. I told her to wait until they had a few entertainment contracts, but she's ready to commit."

Frank looked at his partner for a moment, his bottom lip protruding in a way that Logan had come to learn meant trouble. "That sounds awfully protective to me so I'm going to guess that somehow you've managed to break through the well-known Justine Hart resistance. Am I correct?" he asked.

"I have no idea what you're talking about," Logan responded, ending the questions but not for long, he suspected. To further make his point and get back to work in a way that would be obvious even to the persistent Frank, he picked up the telephone.

Frank wasn't fazed. "You know, now that we've got her signed, I have another idea," he said, ignoring the telephone ploy.

Logan looked at him over the rim of his glasses and, with a shrug, put down the phone. "I have a feeling you're going to tell me just what it is."

"You got it. On the subject of La Quinta entertainers, suppose we talked to her manager, Adele Schwartz, and arranged a singing engagement there for Justine? Maybe a week's booking. If she doesn't have that kind of time available, even a day or two would guarantee that the club would be a success. It would be helpful to her, to our other clients—"

"And to us?"

"Of course," Frank answered with a grin.

Logan shook his head. "I don't think so."

"Why not, for God's sake? Everyone would benefit. I thought it was a pretty bright idea. In fact, I've been congratulating myself for thinking about it ever since I heard you two were safe."

Logan laughed. "Now, if we'd been dead, that might have presented a problem."

"Logan, I *knew* you weren't dead."

"Don't tell me you also have a guru?"

"What?"

"Never mind," Logan said with a smile. "How'd you know I wasn't dead?"

"Just couldn't happen," Frank responded, pointing to the desk. "Too much work was piling up. Now about Justine singing at La Quinta. I'm sure you'll be seeing her again, and so you can—"

"Nope. I won't use my personal relationship with Justine."

"So there is a personal relationship! I thought as much." Frank settled more comfortably in the chair, prepared for a lengthy discussion on the merits of Justine Hart.

He was in for a surprise. "Get back to your office, Frank," Logan said with a stern look. "We both have a lot of work to do."

Frank sat openmouthed before shaking his head and saying, "Damn. It's serious between you two."

"I'm getting ready to throw something, Frank."

"I'm leaving, I'm leaving," Frank assured his partner. "I just never imagined staid, old Logan Addison..."

"Frank—"

"Okay, okay. But bring her to the wedding, pal, so Diane and I can both have a good look at you two together and make up our own minds. I'm getting married, you know."

"I know, Frank. Out," Logan demanded, and watched with a grin as his partner finally complied. As soon as Frank was safely out of the office and on his way down the hall, Logan picked up the phone, but not to make a business call. This was one of many attempts to reach Justine. He'd tried her private number first, gotten a recording and left a message on the machine. Then he'd tried her answering service and left another message. Finally he'd called Adele, whose secretary had less information than the machine or the service. Now he was starting all over.

He didn't reach her until after midnight the next day. Justine had just come in from rehearsal, turned off her answering machine without playing back the messages and headed for the shower when the phone began ringing. She thought about ignoring it. She knew who it was, and she'd avoided returning his calls for a reason. Justine was painfully aware that once they got together, her prediction would be proven true: They'd never be able to make it as a couple. Not seeing him allowed her to continue the fantasy, hoping maybe she was wrong.

Logan was persistent, thinking that if the machine wasn't turned on, she must be home. He let the phone ring until, finally, Justine turned off the shower and reached for it.

"I thought you'd left the country and headed back to St. Cat's," Logan said with calculated casualness.

"Oh, I'd like to." Justine walked across the bathroom into her dressing room, trailing the phone cord along, and stretched out on a comfortable chaise in front of her wall-to-wall closet. "It's been a hectic day." In the mirrored door of the closet, she could see her reflection. Some of the tan from St. Cat's was still there but none of the rested, relaxed demeanor that she'd seen only yesterday.

"I've been trying to reach you for two days. For a woman with so many numbers, you're pretty hard to get hold of."

"I just walked in from the studio," she explained. "The rehearsal was really a hectic affair, a mess, actually," she decided. "We tape tomorrow, and I'm not sure I can do it."

"Of course you can, Justine. You'll be terrific. Remember, I've heard you sing in person," he said with a touch of familiarity, "so I should know."

She didn't pick up on the personal tone. "I'm just too tired even for a smile," she told him, "and frankly, I'm scared, Logan."

He was glad to hear her admit that feeling, and somehow it made them closer. "Why, Justine?" he asked.

"Oh, all the usual reasons: TV's not really my medium, I haven't done a special in a long time, I feel like I have to prove myself all over again. I always have at least three days to rehearse, usually four. I'm not sure I can do it with only two days." She was letting him see her uncertainty, maybe because she'd let him see so much else about her on St. Cat's.

"You're a pro, Justine," he assured her. "You'll bring it off beautifully."

"I hope you're right. I just don't want to let them down."

"Who?"

"The orchestra, my back-up singers, the crew, everyone who's worked so hard. Often when a singer gets to be a big star, it's undeserved. Some of them aren't very talented, and when they do a special like this, the other performers have to carry them, make them look good. Do you know what I mean?"

"Yes," Logan said, "but you're not in that category, Justine. You have real talent, and you're going to be great, I'm sure of it. When you get out there and the lights come up, they'll all see the real star."

"I hope so."

"Now, when can I see you?" he asked.

"Not until it's all over," Justine answered.

"I'll be at the taping," he told her.

"No," she said, "it's not going to be in front of a live audience. It's a closed taping, and they aren't letting anyone in. I'll meet you afterward."

That didn't suit Logan. "I don't want to take a chance on someone else sweeping you away. I'll come by and pick you up at the studio. What's the address?"

"Logan, I'm really not sure they'll let you in."

"Just let them try and stop me."

She'd been right about one thing—they weren't remotely interested in letting him into the television studio. He was only one of a crowd of fans trying to get past the guard at the stage door. How they all knew about the taping, Logan couldn't imagine. There must be a sixth sense among the celebrity groupies, he decided as he brushed past them, announced himself to the guard, showed his business card, declared that he was Miss Hart's financial advisor and would be accompanying her to dinner that evening. He said it all in one authoritarian breath, at the same time slipping the man a folded bill.

Logan couldn't be sure whether it was the aura of authority or the color of his money that got him through the door, and once inside he wasn't sure what to do next. He found himself in a long, dimly lit corridor. Overhead he could hear the thud of an orchestra playing. It was nine o'clock, just the time when Justine had expected to be finished. Obviously they were going over. He reached the end of the hall, where a spiral staircase led to the next floor. He climbed it, his footsteps echoing hollowly on the iron steps. At the top was a door. He pushed it open.

This was the right place, Logan decided. There was no doubt about that. The dressing rooms along the hall were filled with costumed performers, waiting for their call. The sounds of the orchestra were louder, and he could even hear Justine's voice.

"Excuse me." He stopped the most normal-looking one in the large group. "Can you tell me where Justine Hart—"

"She's on stage." The man was dressed in black sequined shirt and pants and had applied the mascara a bit heavily, Logan thought.

"I know that. I'd just like to wait for Miss Hart. If you can tell me where her dressing room is."

The response was a disinterested lifting of the chin. "That way. Number three."

The last notes sounded from the orchestra, and a voice at the end of the hall called out, "On stage for the dance number everyone." With a rustle of costume and high-pitched excitement, the halls miraculously cleared. Logan found himself standing outside room number three. On a small white card tacked to the door was penciled, *Justine*.

"So much for star treatment," Logan said aloud as he pushed through into the dressing room.

He waited there an hour, and as he waited Logan began to find himself worrying about what was happening on the stage, how Justine was doing. He'd never for a moment doubted that she was a pro, but he hadn't actually seen her perform, he'd only heard the results on recordings. She'd been nervous about this taping, and because of their adventure on St. Cat's, she'd missed two full days of rehearsal. That certainly would make a difference in anyone's performance, he realized.

Then he thought about her fears, her uncertainties that had begun when she was just a child, prompted by her mother's negativism. Every available space in her dressing room was filled with flowers, including the bouquet he'd sent that he couldn't identify in the vast assortment that cluttered the room. Even surrounded by the evidence of so many well-wishers, Logan could still feel the uncertainty that must have nagged at Justine before she went onstage. He'd reassured her, told her that she would be fabulous as usual, but now he wished that he'd been with her before she went on to hold her and give her the confidence she needed.

Suddenly Logan realized that the sound of the music had ended. There was a momentary silence followed by a cacophony of noises that continued for a full twenty minutes before the door finally opened and Justine slipped inside. She didn't see him for the first moment as she leaned against the door with an expression on her face that was a mixture of elation and relief. Looking at her, he shared that relief.

"Well, it's over and it was great, I can tell," he said, standing up to greet her.

"Oh, Logan, I—"

"Had you forgotten that I said I'd be here?"

"Of course not. I'm glad to see you," she answered as he kissed her lightly on the cheek, "but I'm afraid I'm a mess in all this makeup and I'm perspiring so..." She sat down at the dressing table and dabbed at her face with a tissue before reaching for a large jar of cold cream.

"You look wonderful," he said, touching her tentatively on the shoulder.

"Thank you." Justine covered his hand with her own briefly and then smiled up at him. At first he thought the smile was for him. Then he saw it reflected in the mirror and knew it was the smile of a star. "I'll just take off my makeup and then change out of my costume..."

Logan realized that he was making her uncomfortable and offered, "Maybe I should wait outside."

She seemed relieved. "If you don't mind."

"You *will* have dinner with me?"

"Of course," she said, adding, "as long as I can get back by midnight."

"Back here?"

"Yes, they'll have the tape ready for us to see."

By *us*, Logan realized she meant the other members of her show. "Fine," he said, glancing at his watch. "I'll just wait outside. Do hurry, Justine. We only have two hours."

"Logan, I told you—"

"Just hurry," he repeated as he went out into the hall, closing the door behind him and immediately berating himself for having been so sharp with her. This was Justine's night; naturally she would want to see the tape. He'd just have to make the most of his two hours. Logan smiled wryly to himself; this wasn't the most auspicious beginning, waiting outside her dressing room like a Stage-door Johnny.

It got worse. Justine emerged, wearing an outfit wilder than the one he'd first seen her in at the Miami airport, including her red sunglasses. She stopped to greet all the members of her company, accept their congratulations and offer her thanks. Getting through that crush was nothing compared to working their way from the stage door to a cab through the waiting fans with their autograph books.

Justine looked up at Logan with a shrug that admitted defeat and reached for one book after the other as they made their way to the cab.

A fan, overly zealous, bumped against Logan, offered his book and asked, "Are you someone?"

"You're damned right I am," Logan shot back, taking the book and scrawling his name across a full page.

Another half hour passed before they finally reached their destination, a small Italian restaurant where the quiet, elegant setting was a relief after the charged up atmosphere they'd just escaped. Logan found himself breathing a sigh. Everything would be all right here. Here he was known.

"How good to see you again, Mr. Addison," the maître d' greeted. "We have a table ready for you. This way, please."

As soon as they sat down and ordered, an awkwardness came over them. If Logan hadn't expected that, Justine certainly had. Their battle through crowds had at least been diverting. Now here they were, sitting across from each other with nothing to say. He asked a few polite questions about her show, and she gave a few polite answers. This was the man with whom she'd made passionate love, Justine thought, giving herself with such abandon, but the magic was gone, not to be recaptured. This was the real world, and just as she'd predicted, they didn't belong in it together.

That knowledge didn't prevent her from trying to recapture something of the old feelings. Even though she knew it was fading, she still wanted to hold on to what they'd once had. Maybe, just maybe—

Then it happened. A couple leaving the restaurant walked past their table and recognized Justine. They were polite and almost apologetic for bothering her at dinner to ask for an autograph. Yet bother her they did, and Logan couldn't restrain his anger.

"Do you always have to sign autographs?" he asked when the couple left, "Even during meals?"

She nodded. "I try not to ever turn anyone down. Do you mind?"

"Yes, I think I do. I've been looking forward to this evening together, brief as it must be, and having you to myself. I didn't expect to share you with every groupie in New York."

"I told you it would be like this, Logan. I told you it wouldn't be the same as on St. Cat's."

"Well, congratulations," he said bitterly, "you were right." Logan felt his frustration and anger boiling up inside and stopped to take a deep breath. It didn't help. His next remark was just as bitter. "Maybe this is not only what you predicted, Justine, but what you wanted." He didn't give her time to deny that. "Well, it's certainly not what I wanted or what I planned."

"What did you plan, Logan? There're no palm trees here, and there's no blue lagoon. This is New York, not St. Cat's." She reached over and touched his hand and tried to make him understand. "I'm glad to see you, but in a way I think this might have been the wrong time with all the chaos surrounding my taping, not to mention the publicity about me—about us—in the papers. Maybe we should have waited until that story died down a little more."

"Afraid I'll damage your image?" It was a vague attempt at a joke.

But Justine was serious. "No, I was actually thinking about your reputation."

He eyed her a little warily but knew she was serious and felt a pang of regret over his remark.

"I'm sure your clients aren't going to be impressed by this much-publicized romance. Even if some of them are show business people," she told him, "they're still serious investors who depend on a serious financial advisor."

Neither of them had touched the pasta dishes Logan had ordered. Justine made a vague attempt to eat a little before adding, "I think we need to be apart for a while so we can do some serious thinking."

"No," he insisted. "We need to be together to bring back what happened on the island, and we *can* bring it back. It's still there, just below the surface. Let's not step away and let it fade. Let's take the time, Justine," he pleaded.

"We might not have it, Logan," she said. "I'm due back at the studio at midnight. Then I have to fly out to LA in the morning to tape the Carson show. On Friday I'm doing a benefit in San Francisco. Then back to New York—"

"I see what you mean," Logan interrupted. There was as much hurt as anger in his eyes.

"That's just the way it is."

"No," he corrected, "that's the way you want it. That's what you predicted. I didn't believe it then, and I still don't. Yes, we're very different; yes, our worlds are very far apart, but it doesn't have to be that way.

We could make it work if both of us wanted to badly enough. We could *find* the time."

"I can't change my life, my career, my whole way of coping because, just because—"

"Of a fling on an island with—what did the papers call me? 'The stuffy scion of a well-to-do family'? Come on, Justine," he said, pushing his plate aside and standing up. "It's eleven-thirty. We better start back now in case we encounter more of your enthusiastic fans."

Justine had a sudden placating thought. "Why don't you come to the studio with me to watch the tape? I'm sure they wouldn't mind."

"I don't think so, Justine. I'll wait and see it on TV with the rest of your public."

Chapter Seven

Justine returned to her apartment on the East Side of New York three hectic days later, exhausted but elated. Beginning with the midnight viewing of her television show, everything had gone well for her, remarkably well. The show, which she'd had such misgivings about and which had taken an hour longer to tape than expected, was good. She'd known that as soon as the last note of the last song was sounded. She just hadn't known *how* good, and the two-hour interval with Logan had put a damper on everything. When she'd gotten back to the studio, she almost hadn't cared what she saw on the screen.

Then what she saw jolted her. Even if she'd been watching alone, Justine would have picked up on the vitality and that certain spark that happens so infrequently, almost never in a taped show with no audience. It was there in her show, however, an electricity between Justine and the other performers, a quality when she stood alone on the stage that she hadn't felt in a long time. She'd felt it that night at the taping, but she'd been wary of it, afraid it was misleading. It wasn't. By the time the tape ended, the whole room was cheering, shouting, even crying over the show.

Riding high on that, Justine had left for the West Coast, stopping first in Los Angeles to do the Carson show. She was usually effective in that kind of format, singing one number, maybe two, and then joining him for a few minutes of talk about herself. There'd been a time, years before, when she'd found being "on" in that way embarrassing. Now she did it almost as second nature. With her red sunglasses and her outlandish costumes, things just seemed to *happen* on talk shows. This one had been no exception.

She'd gone on to the benefit in San Francisco, and she'd had a marvelous time both onstage and off, particularly because Adele had flown out for two days and they'd made a holiday of it, exploring, shopping in stores they'd never seen before, taking a chance on restaurants just because they looked interesting, discovering marvelous food and as Adele said, "Adding new experiences along with pounds." But worth it all, somehow.

Only when she got back and let herself into a dark empty apartment did Justine realize that she'd had a little ache inside during all the days she'd been gone. Working hard and playing hard, she'd managed to avoid thinking about it, about *him*.

As soon as she put her suitcase down, Justine went to the phone, first calling her service for messages and then playing back the tape on her answering machine, the whole time knowing the message she wanted wouldn't be there, but still hoping. Uselessly hoping as it turned out. He hadn't called. But wedged in among all the messages, there *was* one that served to lift her spirits a little and momentarily gladdened her heart. She returned the call immediately.

"Carter, how marvelous to hear your voice. I had no idea you'd be in New York so soon."

"It wasn't really planned, my dear. I just had a sudden urge to see my favorite singer. I'll be here all day tomorrow, and I hope to spend it with you, if you're free."

She wasn't. Her schedule was full, but she wanted to talk with him if only over the phone.

"Problems?" Carter asked, noticing her moment of hesitation.

"Yes, problems. I have a million things to do. I'm running around like a crazy person."

"One more reason for you to take some time off. Call it a mental health day for your sanity." Then as an added inducement he said, "I'm only here for two days."

"I'll get myself free somehow," Justine decided. "I can't wait, Carter." She couldn't, not just because of Carter but because of the rush of memories he brought with him, memories of St. Cat's and the times that *were*. She wanted to recapture them. She needed to recapture them.

"Fine," he said with relief. "Let's begin by doing something outside in the crisp autumn air. I do so enjoy putting on an overcoat and remembering what it's like to feel a chill in the air. Very invigorating—in small doses," he added. "What about the zoo?"

"Sounds like fun."

"Can you make yourself unrecognizable to the crowds?"

"Not guaranteed," Justine admitted, "but if I wear a wool cap and a big overcoat, there's a chance of anonymity."

"Marvelous. Now, shall we tell Logan about this little outing or shall we wait and include him in dinner plans only, so I can have you to myself for a while?"

"Have you talked to Logan yet?" Justine asked carefully.

"No, I decided to find out what was up with you first."

"Then I think it would be best if you saw us separately." Justine's voice was a little shaky. She wasn't quite sure how to handle this and almost wished Carter had called Logan and put the onus on him. "Maybe lunch with one of us and dinner with the other," she suggested, adding, "but do save the afternoon at the zoo for me."

"Of course," Carter assured her, his words followed by a thoughtful silence. "I must add my surprise, however, Justine. During the afternoon we spent together at Savoy's Revenge, I had the distinct impression that you and Logan were much more than business associates. I particularly had that feeling the night before when I watched you two from afar. I'm not usually wrong about that sort of thing, but frankly, any fool could have seen there was something between you. Not even a fortnight has passed since then...."

"It's not the time that's important, Carter. It's the place. That was St. Cat's; this is New York."

"Don't tell me there's something about New York that precludes romance. I've always heard otherwise," he said in what Justine understood as an attempt to lighten the conversation.

She couldn't keep the mood going because she felt a need to let Carter know, firmly and finally, that she *was* serious. She didn't want to see Logan during Carter's visit any more than Logan would have wanted to see her. What fantasies might accompany the time she spent with Carter, what memories, were her secret. Neither Carter nor Logan would ever have to know about them.

"For others, this may be a very romantic place," she said, "but for Logan and me it's just home, where our lives and our separate, very separate, careers are. We don't see each other here," she said, and because Carter was a man of sensitivity the subject was closed.

The next day *was* cloudy and cold. "I hope you're happy," Justine told Carter as they walked through Central Park after their visit to the zoo. "This is just the overcoat weather you wished for."

"But enough is enough," he responded, taking her arm and turning her back in the direction they'd come from. "Where's the nearest taxi?"

After spending the rest of the afternoon in a museum that was, Carter observed, both thought provoking and *warm*, they separated briefly to dress for dinner. Carter's favorite restaurant wasn't one of the expensive haunts of the social crowd but was chic enough to keep any possible fans at a distance.

After a quiet dinner they headed for Carter's hotel. "I've monopolized most of your day," Justine said as they rode uptown in the cab. "It's probably Logan's turn by now." That was the first mention of Logan, and just speaking his name made her suddenly tense.

Carter must have sensed that, Justine decided, for his response was brief, "Logan's for later; now is for Justine. I have a piano in my suite. Will you sing for me?"

Justine glanced at her watch. She had a full schedule the next day, beginning very early. Since she'd returned from St. Cat's, Justine had quickly gotten back into the habit of sleeping late. Tomorrow would be a struggle even if she went home immediately and went right to bed.

"There's one problem, Carter," Justine said. "I have a breakfast meeting in the morning, and if I don't get to sleep soon, I'll barely be able to drag myself to it which will make my manager very angry, to put it mildly."

Carter reached over and took Justine's hand. "Answer me honestly now, Justine, since you are, I very strongly suspect, a night person like myself. If you go home now will you go to bed and to sleep? Truthfully," he cautioned.

Justine laughed. "No, of course not. I never go to sleep until after midnight no matter what time I have to get up. So let's go find that piano and harmonize a little."

"My thoughts exactly. You've yet to be entertained by my most unusual voice."

It *was* an unusual voice and a very delightful one. After Justine sang one or two of the numbers from her new show for him, Carter sang and played for her by ear, with a touch that he called, "Short on mastery and long on chords." Then Justine joined him in duets that they assured each other were quite wonderful. "If a record company executive were here tonight, he'd sign us up on the spot," Carter commented.

"You should have been on the stage."

"It was enough to write for it, my dear," he said. "My temperament wasn't adequate to perform. I'm too lazy and not *quite* vain enough."

"In that case, what about a little Cole Porter?"

"Done." Once more their voices blended in harmony, each song leading to "just one more" that was a favorite.

The performance part of their evening ended with a bawdy song Carter had learned at a Brighton music hall fifty years earlier. Laughing until they were close to tears, he and Justine moved into the living room with their glasses of brandy.

"Oh, I meant to tell you that I stopped by La Quinta for a second look. I'm definitely going to invest."

"You liked it that much?" Justine kicked off her shoes and curled up on the sofa.

"It's actually quite stunning. Sometimes those public resorts can be just a little, shall we say, *déclassé*. This one is exceptionally tasteful. Every detail has been thought out carefully. Very nice," he summarized.

"I thought so, too," Justine agreed.

"However..." Carter sipped his brandy and relaxed at least to the extent that he ever allowed himself to relax. He didn't take off the jacket of his tuxedo or even loosen his bow tie, but he put his feet, clad in patent leather dress shoes, up on a footstool and leaned back on the sofa pillows.

"However, what?"

Carter shrugged. "I spent a little time poking around, listening to the gossip." He took another sip of his brandy.

"What did you find out?" she asked, a little nervous now, especially since she was a committed investor in La Quinta.

"Well, nothing that would make me change my mind. However, I certainly plan to check with Logan, because rumor has it that reservations are running behind the initial projections."

"Really? The man who showed us around said that in no time people would be turned away."

Carter smiled. "Naturally, it's in his best interest to say just that. All they need, apparently, is to book the first few weeks with top talent in order to attract attention. After that, they'll have no problems since it is, as I said, such an outstanding club. But they need talent. Have they contacted you?" he asked.

Justine shook her head. "Haven't been booked, haven't been asked, haven't even been approached." It was a little disquieting, the thought that reservations weren't pouring in as Señor Ortego had assured.

"Could be just a rumor," Carter said unperturbed, as he rotated his brandy glass.

"Yes, that's true, but if it isn't, I certainly would like to be informed. I'd consider playing a date there if only to help out my own investment," she said, wondering why Logan hadn't called her about the club. Well, she knew why Logan hadn't called, but why hadn't she heard from Frank—or *someone* at Norwood and Addison?

"You've heard nothing from Logan?"

Justine shook her head.

"Neither personal nor business?"

"No," she said softly.

"Tell me, Justine, I didn't misread what I sensed between you and Logan on St. Cat's, did I?"

"No," Justine answered. "You didn't misread it."

"Then may a nosy old man inquire what happened in the intervening ten days?"

She shook her head in resignation. It seemed there was no way, short of rudeness, to avoid talking about Logan. "Nothing happened, Carter. Except maybe life—life happened," she answered.

"And what, may I ask, was that you were experiencing on St. Cat's if not life?"

"A dream. A fantasy. I wasn't myself on the island and neither was Logan."

"Now that you're back in New York, you're totally...yourselves," Carter said with a smile that was, possibly, a little disbelieving.

Justine tried to explain. "I knew all along that it couldn't work, that we weren't right for each other."

"Did Logan know?"

"Not right away, but he does now. He's learned," she said almost bitterly. Justine had the sudden urge to tell Carter what had happened on the one evening they'd spent together, but she changed her mind. That wasn't something she wanted to discuss. She hadn't even told Adele. Of course, her manager knew very well the kind of life Justine led, knew very well that it didn't fit with Logan's life and never would. She didn't have to tell Adele.

"Well, I am sorry," Carter said sincerely. "I like you separately, of course, but we did have such fun, the three of us together."

"Yes, we did," Justine responded, remembering and then berating herself for remembering and silently admonishing Carter for making her remember. She put her glass down on the table and attempted a smile. "It's been lovely, Carter, the whole day, but it really is time for me to leave."

"Do you think you'll sleep now?"

"Yes, I think I will."

"In that case...but only if you insist." Carter stood up reluctantly and was on the way to the closet to retrieve her coat when the doorbell rang.

He looked over at Justine and smiled. It was a smile she hadn't seen before, one that was half embarrassed and half pleased. "I won't say, 'Now who can that be?' even though it was one of the more frequently spoken lines in my drawing room comedies. However, I will say, 'He's early.'" Before Justine could reply, Carter was on his way down the long hall toward the door.

She heard his voice before she saw him, felt his presence before he stepped into the room. By the time he appeared, she was ready for him. She'd prepared a defense against the magnetism of him, but when he came closer, the preparation crumbled away.

Like Carter, he was wearing a tuxedo. There the resemblance ended. No one looked quite like Logan

Addison in dinner clothes. The white studded shirt-front made his face seem that much more tan. He wasn't wearing his glasses, and his blue eyes flashed against the golden brown skin. His hair looked darker than ever, almost as black as the tux that fit him perfectly but which he wore with a casualness that only someone who'd been born to wear such clothes could achieve. He'd taken off his overcoat and hung it in the hall closet, but his white silk scarf was still around his neck.

A look of surprise registered on Logan's face. There could have also been a wariness, even a hostility there, but his innate good breeding wouldn't allow it to show through. Justine knew immediately that this rendezvous had been planned and executed by Carter alone. Logan wasn't involved. She'd have to hand it to Carter; he was certainly a persistent matchmaker. She couldn't blame him for interfering because he didn't know how much of an interference this was. He didn't know the whole story. It was her fault for not telling him about that one and only evening she and Logan had spent together in New York. The evening that proved hopeless and ended in anger.

Since there was nothing else she could do, Justine decided to play along. She would stay and make herself agreeable until an opening occurred that would allow her to leave the two men to themselves.

While Carter fussed around, poured Logan a drink and generally acted nervous, Justine looked at Logan and smiled. That was a mistake. She felt the breath catch in her throat when he returned the smile. Being face-to-face with him wasn't going to be easy.

"You look wonderful, Justine. The trip must have been successful." He seemed perfectly at ease.

"It was. Very." She strove to keep her voice as casual as his. It was his turn now, she thought, to keep up the faltering conversation but he said nothing. He just stood there looking at her. He was waiting for her, and she obliged, filling the silence with a question, that if not brilliant, was at least businesslike.

"I've been wondering about the status of my La Quinta investment. I haven't had a progress report."

His answer was equally businesslike. "You and the other investors will be getting up-to-date information in the mail in the next day or two." Logan accepted a glass of brandy from Carter, who was choosing to remain silent, at least, Justine imagined, until she and Logan ran into a conversational snag.

"I heard the initial interest in the club wasn't quite what Señor Ortego led us to believe." Justine didn't mention her source, and Carter didn't even blink.

"Business is never as good as the publicists would have us think," Logan said. "The club is going to be successful in time, if not immediately. However, a couple of investors who are also entertainers are hot to get rich quick. They're going to play dates at La Quinta to guarantee early crowds."

"Maybe I should consider playing there . . ."

Logan raised one eyebrow, knowing that if Frank was in his place, he'd jump right onto that suggestion. But Frank wasn't there, and Logan didn't want to suggest or even agree. "You could talk to Adele about it and see what she thinks."

"Or talk to Frank," Justine said. "I imagine he would be in favor of the idea."

"Yes, I imagine so," Logan responded.

The silence that Carter seemed to be waiting for descended upon them, bringing him quickly to the rescue. "Well, I for one would very much like to see Justine at La Quinta and for selfish reasons. It would bring her close to me. From there I could lure her back to St. Cat's and collect that promised visit. Your pilot has returned, by the way, the one who deposited you so precipitously onto my landing strip."

"Steve?" Justine supplied.

"Exactly. It looks like he's going to be a frequent if not permanent visitor, thanks to Angelique, who has tempted him back to us. Quite a romantic story, eh?"

Logan was watching Justine. She could feel his eyes, but she couldn't meet them.

Carter forged ahead. "Angelique works for the staff at Savoy's Revenge occasionally. A very sweet child quite unlike her father, who is the island's most notorious, shall we say, con man?"

"I have a pair of the sandals he makes." Justine could feel Logan's eyes on her again, and she wondered if he was also remembering that first night on St. Cat's when they'd been such strangers. "They cost considerably less at Martin's store," she added, trying to remember no more than that.

"Furthermore," Carter told her, "Monsieur Moreau doesn't even make the sandals. He buys them from another island, where he has a 'contract,' or so he calls it, to import merchandise. Half of what's for sale on St. Cat's finds its way to shops through old Moreau." Carter laughed. "Yes, our island has many interesting characters, all of whom I plan to introduce you to the next time you visit." Carter smiled and poured himself another brandy. "You see, I'm persistent."

Once again, Justine felt Logan's eyes on her as if he were waiting for a reply. When it wasn't forthcoming, Logan answered. "I plan to take you up on the invitation, Carter, if only for a long weekend so I can do some snorkeling and spearfishing."

"We have just the reefs for it," Carter encouraged.

"I know," Logan agreed. "I saw them, but we didn't have time for everything while we were there."

Justine tried not to look at him, for fear that he would be able to interpret what she was thinking—that they'd only had time for falling in love. Almost.

"We could take my boat out for some sailing, as well," Carter tempted, and as he and Logan got into a spirited discussion on the subject, Justine suddenly visualized Logan on the prow of a sailboat, the wind blowing in his hair, his eyes searching the sea. She tried to shake away the vision when another one took its place, one even more provocative, Logan diving from the boat, his long muscular body entering the water cleanly without leaving a ripple and then reappearing just below the surface of the clear blue sea. She felt a painful ache inside, a loneliness for what might have been, which caused her to stand up suddenly.

"At the risk of repeating myself," she directed toward Carter, "I must say that I've enjoyed our day together, but this time I really have to leave." She couldn't stand being here any longer, so close to Logan and yet so far from him.

"You'll be able to sleep?" Carter asked.

"Absolutely."

Carter saw Logan's perplexed look and explained, "Justine is a night person, like myself, who goes to sleep in the wee hours of the morning and doesn't rise until noon if possible."

Logan knew better because he'd seen her in the glow of sunrise, but when he tried to catch Justine's eye to share that secret, she looked away as she'd done all those other times during the evening. Obviously anxious to leave quickly, she had already started down the hall with the two men following. At the door she kissed Carter on the cheek, slipped into the coat he held, shook Logan's hand and was quickly out the door and on the way to the elevator.

Justine was just about to expel a breath of relief that she'd escaped whatever danger the hotel suite held, when Logan appeared beside her. His hand reached out to press the elevator button.

"You didn't think Carter and I would let you walk out into the night alone, did you?"

Justine looked around for Carter.

"He decided not to come with us," Logan said, grinning. As they entered the elevator his hand fit lightly under her elbow. "Did our stories about sailing bore you so much?"

"No, I..." Justine searched for an excuse all the way down in the elevator, across the lobby and out into the brisk night. Then she plunged from the safety of the lie that she'd almost voiced to the danger of truth.

"Seeing you and Carter brought back so many memories of St. Cat's." She should have stopped there, but she didn't. That truth seemed to allow room for more. "I could almost smell the fragrance of flowers and the salt of the sea. I could almost feel the breeze. Those memories were painful, and I wanted to get away from them.''

''I don't think it's possible to outrun memories,'' Logan observed. ''They're painful for me, too, especially when we aren't together. That was what you wanted, though, wasn't it?'' A cab pulled up near them, but he waved it away, lodged his hand more deliberately under her arm and began walking.

The cold autumn night was just what Justine had been looking forward to, but she hadn't expected to share it with Logan. It didn't clear her head as she had hoped it would, not with him beside her.

''Yes, that's what I wanted,'' she agreed, answering his question long after it was asked.

''You never thought we could make it, Justine. You never had faith in us.''

''I know. That was because I was scared. I'm still scared,'' she admitted, looking up at him and seeing his strong profile in the street light. They were walking north on Fifth Avenue, but Justine didn't notice that, as she didn't notice the scattering of people who walked past them, the cabs cruising by or the occasional bus. She only saw Logan and thought only about him. ''I didn't give us a fair chance,'' she murmured, and then almost hoped he hadn't heard her.

They walked in silence, Logan never commenting on what she'd said, Justine not knowing whether he'd heard or not. When he stopped walking and turned to her, she realized that they were in front of her apartment building.

''Yes,'' he said, answering her silent question. ''I know where you live—and for how long, and the amount of maintenance you pay. Remember, we handled the purchase of your penthouse at Norwood and Addison.''

For a moment Justine didn't respond. Then she heard herself say, ''In that case, maybe you should come up and see what you bought for me.''

Through the door, across the lobby, past the doorman and the elevator man and the other tenants without a glance, Logan led Justine, not pausing, not speaking until they were inside the door of her penthouse apartment.

''So here we are.''

''Yes, here we are,'' she echoed. He noted the little nervous tremor in her voice and decided not to do anything to put her at ease. There'd be no light, bright and airy conversation about the light, bright and airy art deco furnishings in her apartment, no conversation about anything.

''Would you like a drink?'' she asked. The danger that she'd felt in Carter's hotel suite from that first moment when she heard his voice had grown more and more intense until she'd admitted her feelings to him in a voice barely audible. The danger was past. There was nothing to fear in the feelings that surged through her now.

''No, I wouldn't like a drink.''

He looked down at her standing beside him. She was all the things he remembered—sophisticated, beautiful, tempting and fascinating. All of those words fit her. She was something more tonight, though, something that was for him alone. She was approachable, and she was vulnerable. She'd been honest with him, and that had made her approachable. She'd missed him and told him so, and that had made her vulnerable. She was also brave—she'd told him how she felt. Logan wasn't sure he could do the same, not because he was afraid to admit his feelings but because there wouldn't be time now that they were a step away, a breath away.

There wasn't time to say it all or even some of it. There was barely time to say her name, "Justine."

His arms were around her, and he felt as if he'd always been holding her, as if she'd never left him. How good, he thought, how right to be holding her again. Justine in his arms, Justine with her lips on his, Justine putting her arms around his neck, returning his kiss with all the passion in her heart. Her breasts were crushed against the front of his shirt, her thighs molded into his. She was part of him. She was his.

Still kissing, still holding each other, they crossed the foyer, down the stairs into the living room and along the hall to her bedroom. There was a lamp beside her bed, but she didn't reach for it. A dim light from the hall filtered through the room and gave all the illumination they needed.

Their shadows, dark forms, played along the bare wall, Justine and Logan, moving toward the bed, merging, separating, blending again, one into the other. The shadows wavered, flickered, widened, elongated as they undressed, still in and out of each other's arms, still kissing, struggling with the formal clothes. Unzipping, unbuttoning, their shadows danced across the wall and then suddenly disappeared.

They'd fallen onto the bed. At last Logan was holding her in his arms with his bare skin pressed against her. How long, Justine thought, since she'd felt his muscles ripple beneath her exploring hands, how long since she'd felt his lips on her throat and cheek and chin, at the soft hollow between her breasts and then finally enclosing the peak of one breast.

As he teased the taut bud with his tongue and teeth, Justine rewarded him with little moans of pleasure that escaped from her lips and with her desperately searching hands along his back, down his waist to his hips. Her hands roamed, seeking fulfillment as her lips sought it, her whole body longing to be complete with him.

"Let me kiss you," she murmured when at last he raised his face to hers. "Let me kiss you and love you the way you've loved me."

As Logan lay back on the bed, she used her tongue to tease him and tantalize him, tracing the line of his chin and the column of his neck, the angle of his collarbone to his shoulder, touching and loving him. She tasted her way across his chest until her mouth found his tender nipple, and she gave him the pleasure that he had given her. Looking up at him, Justine saw the smile of excitement on Logan's face. Slowly twisting and turning, she pulled herself along his body until her lips were on a level with his and she could drink of his mouth just as she'd drunk of the rest of him. She ran her tongue along his bottom lip and then his top lip, raining little kisses from one side of his mouth to the other until a moan escaped his lips.

Logan had had enough. He couldn't stand any more of her tantalizing torture. Almost roughly he turned her over and claimed her mouth with his hungry forceful kiss, pressing her down into the pillows, covering her lips, taking them into his mouth.

The determination of that kiss made her head swim; the potency of it made her body go weak. Just when she thought she couldn't stand it any longer, he tantalized her even more, to the very limit. His hands that had been moving over her body found the swell of her abdomen and moved from there to the soft sweet moistness of her womanhood. Little tremors of shock, electrical impulses she couldn't control, flashed through her, and her whole body spasmed at his touch.

Her reaction was almost too much for Logan. Suddenly he had to be inside her and show her his love. He lifted his lips from hers and looked down on her face, the face that had filled his days and haunted his nights. Now she was here with him again, as eager to be loved as he was to love.

Slowly, sweetly, he entered her, filling her more tenderly than ever before. With his body he showed her his love, and with her body she responded. It was an abiding love, and it gave a dreamlike feeling to their joining as if the two of them were floating high in the clouds, as if their bodies were the secret places where all passion existed. As they moved together toward the pinnacle of desire, they seemed to rise above the clouds and touch the heavens in one glorious, perfect moment that made them one.

The moment ended so slowly that they couldn't be sure when it was over or whether it was with them still. If their bodies were satiated, their emotions were still hungry. Justine snuggled against him, fitting herself along the curve of his body. "Oh, how I've missed you," she murmured. "I never realized how much."

"I knew exactly how much," Logan said, "I measured it during every day that we were apart."

"Bless Carter for bringing us back together," she said, entwining her fingers in his. "What an obvious old matchmaker he is. I do believe he *wrote* that scene at his hotel just as if it were a scene in one of his plays."

"I really didn't know what he was up to," Logan began before adding, "Well, maybe I hoped when he invited me that you'd be there." He leaned over and kissed her lips that were reddened by the force of his earlier kisses. Then he touched her bottom lip with his fingertips. "I've bruised you."

"Hmm," Justine said, a little sexily, eliciting a smile from Logan.

"You know, I don't believe that Carter was acting as much like a playwright when he set up that meeting as like a man."

"What do you mean?"

"He still misses his wife. Remember their plans for a dream house? I believe he had that in mind when he brought us back together."

"Trying to tell us not to waste time?"

"Exactly. So let's don't." He kissed her again. "Promise?"

"I promise but with one request."

"Anything," he said.

"No more 'dates' that bring together Logan Addison, investment counselor and Justine Hart, entertainer. That was a phony evening, Logan."

He nodded silently in the half light. "What can we do about it, that's the question."

She was quiet for a long time before answering thoughtfully, "Maybe we shouldn't date."

"What?" He leaned up on one elbow and looked down at her.

"Oh, I don't mean not see each other. I mean try to forget who we are, at least what our status is."

"And just how will we do that, here in New York, where you're a celebrity of the highest order?"

"By spending time together alone," she said resolutely. "Just like on St. Cat's. We can begin with your coming here for dinner."

"You can cook?"

Justine laughed. "Don't sound so surprised. I'm a marvelous cook. Southern dishes are my specialty. So I'll fix dinner, we'll rent movies or listen to music here in our own world."

"But this isn't the real world, either, Justine. It's just more of St. Cat's."

She twisted around in his arms so she could look up at his face. "That's exactly what I want, my darling. More of St. Cat's."

Chapter Eight

Logan had never spent a more perfect Sunday in his
life. That was the thought he couldn't keep out of his
head, and it amazed him as much as it delighted him.
He'd awoken early, as usual, and left Justine sleeping, successfully resisting the urge to kiss her into
wakefulness. She'd looked tempting, snuggled up
against the chrome headboard of her bed, which
looked to Logan like the front end of an old Cadillac.
Her red curls were tangled, her lips parted and her slim
body curled into a ball that he'd only just unfolded
himself from. He'd let her sleep. Even though Justine
had seen a couple of sunrises in St. Cat's, she was and
would remain a night person; if anyone's schedule
would have to be adjusted, it would be Logan's. At
least on weekends, he'd need to learn how to stay up
late and sleep in her arms.

He hadn't learned yet. After pulling on a pair of cords and a sweater, Logan had gone out for bagels, cream cheese and the *New York Times*. When Justine had finally gotten up, spurred on by his unnecessary rattling of pans in the kitchen, the bagels were toasting and the coffee was perking.

They'd gobbled up the breakfast, read their favorite sections of the *Times*, considered spending the morning going through paperwork, which they'd both allowed to accumulate much too long, and then gotten back into bed to make love again until noon.

At two o'clock they'd finally made themselves honor the well-intentioned promise to get some work done, Justine settled at her gold-and-white lacquered desk by the window going through a stack of correspondence, Logan at the glass-and-chrome table in the dining nook bent over portfolios he'd brought from his office. For over an hour they worked silently, taking time out only to reheat the coffee. Just as Logan expected, it was too strong and too bitter. He pushed his cup aside and noticed that Justine had done the same. For a few lazy moments he thought about putting on another pot but got stuck where he was, not drinking the coffee, not working, just watching Justine.

The pale autumn sunlight filtered through the window and danced in her red hair, and Logan thought that she'd never been more lovely. She was dressed absurdly in a pair of old jeans and one of his shirts, which she'd pulled tightly around her hips and tied in front. She was concentrating intently, and a little frown creased her creamy forehead.

As she shuffled through the mail, designating some for her secretary, some for Adele, putting aside those letters that she would have to answer herself, Logan remained mesmerized. Justine was the consummate businesswoman. She knew what she was doing and she did it well. Years of experience had taught her the importance of this aspect of her work, and even though she had advisors in every area of her complicated life, the ultimate decisions rested with Justine alone. She handled them with expertise. Logan had known this about her from the first time they'd met at Norwood and Addison, but it still impressed him to see her in action.

But this competent, businesslike Justine didn't tell the whole story. The rest was complicated, and her fans certainly wouldn't have any suspicions about it. Under the facade of the sophisticated, successful woman, was that little girl who didn't think she was pretty enough or talented enough or smart enough.

They'd spent other nights together, at her place or his, and he was getting to know and understand Justine Hart. Logan leaned back in his chair, having long ago forgotten about the coffee. He closed the folder he'd been trying to review and thought about what had gone into the making of Justine Hart, her unhappy childhood followed by sudden stardom and the betrayal of trust that had sent her reeling. Only after an in-depth search of herself, careful planning of her life and the selection of those who would be around her in the future had she begun to recover. Yes, she was exceptional.

As he watched Justine shifted slightly. The sunlight seemed to follow her and caress her. With one hand she pushed the curls away from her face and smiled at something she was reading. He felt his heart lunge in his chest. Sitting at the breakfast table with a cup of coffee at his elbow, Logan knew at that moment he was in love with her.

It was the oddest feeling, he thought, when he tried to catch hold of it and analyze it, this feeling of love. He'd never experienced it before, never even come close. And among all her insecurities, Justine didn't think she was lovable! Logan almost laughed aloud. In all his life, with all the women he'd known, there'd never been anyone as lovable as she.

Knowing that he wasn't going to get any more work done but not wanting to interrupt Justine's concentration, Logan finally stopped staring at her and picked up the theater section of the *Times*. It was the section she reached for first—and the one he almost never read. He flipped through it, trying to find something that interested him, only because it interested her. He still couldn't stop himself from looking at her over the newspaper pages.

Finally Justine felt the intensity of his gaze. "Have you been watching me for a long time?" she asked, turning in her chair and putting her bare feet on the desk.

"Only for about an hour," he said, still looking, still enraptured.

"Why didn't you say something?"

"I didn't want to bother you since you were so involved in your work. I just can't seem to get involved in mine."

"So you're reading the theater section?"

Logan laughed and pushed his glasses up on his forehead. "Made more interesting by the fact that you have an ad in here." He held up a page of the *Times*. "For your one woman show. 'Limited seats still available.'"

Justine smiled. "I talked to Adele on Friday, and she's very pleased. They've only run one other ad, and we're almost sold out." Justine crossed her arms over her lap and gave a little sigh.

"But what?" Logan asked.

She smiled. "You noticed the doubts. I've got to get the right combination of songs together, Logan. That's so important. My arranger's working on it, but I want everything to be..."

"Perfect," he threw in, shaking his head in wonder. "If you want perfection, you should write all the songs yourself."

Justine laughed. "I could never do that. I've only written one song in my whole career."

"And it's your best one," he reminded her. "If not for this show, then for the next one, I want you to promise me you'll write a new song."

"I'll try, but it'll have to be..."

"Perfect," he said, and they both laughed. "I've never known such a dedicated perfectionist. Are you as hard on others as you are on yourself?"

"The guys in my band complain a lot."

Logan got up slowly from the table, pushing his chair out of the way as he headed for Justine. "You were pretty hard on me, too, if you remember."

"You put an end to that," she teased.

"Damn right." He lifted her feet from the desk and

drew her into his arms. Logan had a destination in mind, but he forgot it for the moment as he allowed his fingers to drift through her hair and linger on her face. Then he remembered and moved away from her cluttered desk. "Let's go over and sit on that thing you call a sofa."

"I have the distinct impression that you don't like my furniture."

"I'm crazy about it. However, it's not what you'd call comfy and cozy."

They sat down on the sofa, which was long and low with rolled arms and a decorative back, definitely art deco. Logan arranged her as best he could on his lap.

"You're used to all that overstuffed Victorian furniture you grew up with."

"How'd you know?" He kissed her softly.

"I guessed."

"Speaking of what I grew up with, my parents are going to be in town next weekend. I think it's time you met them."

Justine sat bolt upright. "Oh, no. I don't think so, Logan. No," she repeated.

"Why not? You'll love them." Logan reached after her and pulled her down against his chest. "I take that back," he said with a laugh. "My parents aren't exactly what you'd call lovable."

"More like stiff upper lip?"

"Yes," he admitted. "Although my father can be pretty amusing after you get to know him. It's the getting to know part that's difficult. My mother is, well, she's very substantial."

"In weight?" Justine asked with a half giggle.

"No, in worth, importance, whatever it is up there in Westchester County that gives those women status."

"You're not making this sound very easy."

"Actually, it'll be something of a chore, but I think we should do it because," he said, looking her straight in the eye, "you're very important to me, and I want them to meet you."

"Well," she said, "put that way..." Then she had another thought. "How many other women have you put through the torture of meeting your parents?"

"None, actually," he admitted.

"Really?" Justine was surprised. "You mean I'm the first one? None of those cool blondes from *Fortune* 500 families who made their debuts and went to finishing school and—"

"How did you know about the cool blondes?" he asked with a twinkle in his eye.

"Just guessed."

Logan laughed. "Well, it was a good guess. Frank always told me that they weren't for me. I had a feeling he was right, but I never suspected a redheaded bombshell was going to burst into my life."

"They aren't going to like me," Justine declared, cuddling back into his arms as if for reassurance.

"The blondes?"

"No, the parents."

"Oh, they'll like you. You're Justine Hart, after all."

Justine thought about that for a long time before responding. "I hope that won't be the reason they like, or dislike me, Logan. I don't want who I am to have anything to do with their feelings toward me. Or with your feelings toward me," she added in a small voice.

Logan turned her in his arms and looked up at her, an almost hard expression in his eyes. "Don't ever think that," he said sternly before admitting, "Once, centuries ago when I first met you, I confess that who you were impressed me. Even later, when we were on La Quinta, I wasn't unaware that you were the famous Justine Hart. But believe me, I haven't thought about it since. Now that you mention it," he added, "it's time we stop hiding away from who you are. We need to face it, Justine."

She looked at him quizzically, but she knew what he was talking about, and she was still fearful of it.

"The real world, Justine. We're insulated against it here. That's not good. We can't hide away forever. We need to sneak back out there and try the waters again. When my parents are in town, let's go out to dinner. Then when Frank and Diane get married, we'll go out again and really make it public."

Justine cuddled closer, somehow needing the security she found in Logan's arms to protect her against what he was suggesting. She didn't respond because she still wasn't sure they were ready for the real world. "Pretty soon you'll be saying that we have to visit the rest of your family."

"Good idea."

"Your brother in France?"

"Sure. He's a lot easier to get to know than my parents. Besides, a trip to Paris would be fun. We could also fly out to California and visit my other brother and his family."

"Followed by a trip to Texas to meet your sister."

"Of course. After all, Justine, you don't have any family left, and I have more than I need so I'm perfectly willing to share."

"They're all so successful," Justine mused aloud. "It's amazing. And all financiers," she said, remembering what Logan had told her about his sister and brothers. "Your father must be very proud."

"I don't believe any of us ever thought about anything else. Economics, banking, international finance. Those were the subjects at the dinner table from the time we were children. I must say, it's exciting in its own way."

"Even with something like Cabaret La Quinta that's not quite as successful as you'd hoped?"

"That's the thrill of the game, making it work. La Quinta's going to work. Trust me."

"Oh, I trust you," Justine said confidently as Logan wrapped his arms around her. "I'm just wondering whether or not I should appear there. I talked to Adele about it."

Logan was beginning to lose track of the subject since his hand had found its way under the baggy shirt and around to Justine's abdomen. His thumb was just beginning to rub along the bottom of one breast inquisitively. "What did Adele say?" he finally asked.

"The dates work, but that's not what matters. I want your advice, Logan."

"Nope," he said firmly as his other hand began loosening the knot she'd tied in the shirttail. "You've always been firmer about that than I, and now I'm very much of your opinion: our personal and professional lives aren't going to get mixed up. The decision about the cabaret will have to be between Frank and

Adele and you. Finally, of course, it's all your decision."

"It might be fun. I have nothing between the show at Carnegie Hall and the concert tour this spring except my new album. Nothing the last couple of weeks in December."

"What about Christmas?"

She shook her head. "I'm not working over the holidays."

Logan had successfully managed to untie the shirt and was now working on the buttons. "Christmas would be a good time to go to the islands. We'd be in the warm sun while the rest of the world is shivering in the snow. I'd be able to skip all the family festivities for a change."

"You mean you'd miss Christmas with your family and go with me to La Quinta?" Justine finally grew tired of Logan's fumbling with the shirt and unbuttoned it for him and then pulled off the T-shirt he was wearing. "I think I'll do it."

"Hmm," he said. "Do what?" He had her jeans unzipped, and was kissing her hungrily.

"Yes," she mumbled. "That."

"And La Quinta, too?"

"La Quinta, too."

All the confidence that Logan had instilled in Justine with his love and his admiration and his compliments didn't do one bit of good the night of their planned dinner with the Addisons. She looked into the mirror—one of her favorite art deco objects, with a frame shaped by the carved arms of a gold braceleted woman whose turbaned head peeked over the top.

Below was Justine's reflection, and she didn't like what she saw there. She'd discarded all the typical Justine Hart outfits immediately and gotten down to the three remaining dresses that looked somewhat proper, or if not proper, at least civilized.

She'd tried them on and decided she looked ridiculous in all of them. Prim didn't work well on her. She threw the last selection across the bed with the others and picked up the phone.

"Logan, I don't have anything to wear," she moaned into the receiver when he answered.

He start laughing immediately and to Justine's indignation laughed throughout the call, pausing every now and then to remind her of the closet full of clothes.

"They're not right," she declared, "and stop laughing or I'm never going to get through this evening."

"Maybe it's the mirror," he said. "Everything looks a little odd under that lady's gilded stare." When that got no reaction he asked, "What do you want me to tell you, Justine?"

"Whether to dress like them or like myself."

"Like yourself, of course," he said, and then, trying not to laugh again, added, "but not too much like yourself."

"That's no help," she cried. "I'm going to close my eyes and reach into the closet. Whatever my hand touches, that's what I'll wear."

"Great idea," Logan said.

That's exactly what she did, setting a few heads turning when they arrived at the Yale Club an hour

and a half later, but getting no sign of recognition
from the staid crowd. The heads that had glanced her
way rotated back to their meals and companions as if
Justine Hart hadn't actually walked into their dining
room.

Mr. and Mrs. Addison were equally circumspect; in
fact, Justine decided, they looked a little embarrassed, as if it were a real surprise to find a rock star
sitting down at their table in the Yale Club dining
room. They overcame the embarrassment quickly, or
made a great effort to do so, putting Justine at ease
with their good manners and ability to keep the conversation going. It wasn't going to be painful, she realized immediately. That made her relax a little. It
wasn't going to be easy, either, she reminded herself
just as quickly when a question came her way that demanded an answer. The look in Logan's eyes when she
glanced at him said something to the effect that he
hadn't promised her a rose garden. She looked away
and tried to keep a straight face.

The Addisons never mentioned the uproar that had
accompanied Logan and Justine back from St. Cat's,
as it would have been in very poor taste to do so.
"We're just glad you're both safe and sound," Mrs.
Addison assured Justine, using the term "we" to include her husband. She did so throughout the evening without for a moment convincing Justine that
Mr. Addison shared her feelings. He certainly never
echoed his wife's remarks although he was polite to
Justine. She kept waiting for his sense of humor to
surface. It never did.

Mrs. Addison quizzed Justine about where she'd
grown up, her parents and extended family, getting

very little information from her dinner companion, who'd left behind the red clay hills of Georgia, whose parents weren't living and who never heard from any other family members unless they needed money. Justine did the best she could with the interrogation, keeping one ear on the conversation between Logan and his father.

"I can't really see any reason for me to stop by, son," Mr. Addison was saying. "I'm sure your offices are very nice, modern and all that. I know some people who've moved into the new complex, but architecturally, I prefer our building. For a generation, in some cases a century, those old firms have taken care of their clients. There's comfort in the tried and true."

"On the contrary, Dad," Logan said, "I don't think there's anything comfortable in those old buildings."

"You've changed, son," was the response, and there wasn't the slightest doubt that the older man held Justine responsible for that change. Logan considered describing the art deco furniture in Justine's apartment, commenting that his father and Justine had something in common in their choice of uncomfortable furniture. He thought better of the idea, however, and his father continued.

"In the old days, I don't think I would have heard you make disparaging remarks about our firm." The words "our firm," Justine noticed, had a sort of holiness about them.

"I'm not being disparaging now, Dad," Logan assured his father. "But the truth is that those leather chairs and sofas have developed some cracks over the years. Maybe I never remarked on that in the old days, but remember that in the old days I left the firm.''

''Yes, a mistake for which I hold Frank responsible,'' Mr. Addison said, clearly indicating that Logan's most recent mistakes were Justine's responsibility. ''I'm not at all sure about this La Quinta investment, by the way,'' he added with a glance toward Justine just at the moment when she and Mrs. Addison had run out of family conversation.

Something made Justine reach for the gauntlet, and when Logan saw the expression on her face, he let her take it up. ''Have you been to the facilities?'' she asked, knowing full well that Mr. Addison had not. ''It stands up beside any similar club in this country or abroad, and I've seen many of them.''

''I have no doubt of that, Miss Hart,'' he said. They hadn't gotten on a first-name basis, and Justine was quite sure she would never be able to refer to Logan's parents as William and Janice. ''But such clubs are not my idea of good investments.''

''Because they wouldn't be financially sound or because you just wouldn't want them in your client's portfolio?'' Logan asked, taking up the challenge because he knew Justine wasn't going to go so far as to actually argue with his father.

They'd finished the first course and as the waiter whisked away the dishes Mr. Addison contemplated his son's question and Justine contemplated Mr. Addison. He was a large man with his son's coloring but otherwise there was little resemblance. Logan didn't look like either of his parents, and for some reason, that was a relief to Justine.

"Obviously," Mr. Addison answered after careful consideration, "I wouldn't be inclined to include such an investment in a portfolio. Furthermore, I think the profit-loss factor is unproportional."

"About that you're wrong, Dad. The cabaret's going to be a success."

Mr. Addison paused, sampled the asparagus timbale, approved it, took a sip of wine and said, "I wonder that you can be so sure. Even if the facility is unusually attractive, you still have to bring in a crowd," he said with a decidedly distasteful reaction to the word "crowd." "That's going to require an enormous amount of advertising, public relations, marketing, that sort of thing. Costly. Very," he added with assurance.

"We'll get the crowds with a minimum of publicity," Logan said winking at Justine. "I'll tell you how. Justine's going to sing there Christmas week." Without even looking in his father's direction for a response, Logan picked up his fork and cut into his rare roast beef hungrily. He was going to enjoy this meal.

Not until it came to an end and Mr. Addison lit his pipe did Logan's mother grasp the significance of Christmas week and realize that her son would be in the islands with Justine. "What about Christmas in Westchester?" she asked Logan, aghast. "The boys will be there, your sister and her children. Logan, you've never missed Christmas," she reminded him.

Logan leaned over and took his mother's hand. "I'm going to miss this one, Mother," he said, "but I somehow doubt if my absence will even be noticed. You'll have your other three children and all four—no five—grandchildren." He laughed. "Eleven. Even without me, that's the same number as last year! Justine and I will come up the week before Christmas and help you get into the spirit," he added, knowing full well that the words were creating a silent moan within Justine.

"Why did you promise that, Logan?" she asked him later as they headed uptown in a cab. "I'll never survive a day at their house in the country."

Logan was laughing again. He'd laughed a lot that evening, Justine had observed. "Because I knew you'd survive the evening, and if you could survive that, you could survive anything. Granted," he said, "the meal was deadly, although the food was unusually good."

Justine nodded. "I'm not sure I digested it, though. I was so nervous. Oh, Lord, why did I argue with your father about La Quinta?"

"Because you're very bright and also very gutsy. Don't fool yourself Justine, he was impressed. Although I must admit he evidenced a definite lack of humor tonight."

"Yes, I kept waiting for him to say something funny."

"Maybe by December," Logan offered with another laugh. "Mother behaved well. She even came over to your side later."

It had been *later* that saved Justine. At the elder Addisons' suggestion, they'd gone to the Carlyle Hotel piano bar to hear a talented entertainer play and sing old standards. "I don't think your parents expected me to appreciate Irving Berlin and Cole Porter," Justine said.

"Not only that, they certainly didn't expect you to be able to sing them. It was a real coup for us when you got invited to join in. You were fabulous, by the way," he added.

Justine was somewhat placated and didn't worry about it anymore—at least not until late that night in bed when she suddenly asked, "Why did I wear that dress? Of all the outfits my hand had to fall on, it would have been that black-and-yellow dress with those crazy designs that made me look like a—"

"Rock star," Logan finished for her as he reached up and pulled Justine back into his arms.

"Ohh," Justine moaned, "a rock star. And one with no family—or none that I want to talk about. We're so *different*, Logan."

"Thank God for that. Besides, Justine, family doesn't matter. Accomplishment is all that matters, and you know it."

Intellectually, she did know but emotionally she was still having a hard time dealing with it. Justine held tightly to Logan and tried to get some of his confidence from the hug, but she still couldn't help wondering if she'd ever be able to forget about where she came from and concentrate on where she was now.

"Besides," Logan added, "you actually get along with my parents as well as I do. Frankly, Justine, they don't have much to do with my life now that I'm an adult," he said with a twinkle in his eye. "Besides, from now on, it's just you and me."

"And the rest of the world," she reminded him. "Remember that we've decided to go public."

"That's right. And we got rid of the hardest part first. After weathering an outing as a couple with my family, getting together with friends is going to be easy. What's your decision about the wedding?''

She was quiet and during that time he leaned over to kiss her. Justine kissed him back enthusiastically.

"Hmm," Logan said, "that was definitely a *yes*."

If the Sunday they'd shared two weeks before had been Logan's best day, the Sunday of Frank and Diane's wedding was high on Justine's list. Diane was a New York businesswoman, an advertising executive who'd struggled to get to the top in what was still basically a man's world. When it came to her wedding, however, she was strictly traditional, not only wearing a long white bridal gown but including her nieces as flower girls and her nephew as ring bearer in a formal service at The Little Church Around the Corner.

Justine went shopping the week before and found a dress that would be just right for the wedding and not call attention to herself. "I don't want anyone to look at me on Diane's day," she told Logan as she put the finishing touches on her makeup. She'd dressed up the long-sleeved navy lamb's wool with a ruffle-collared blouse and a leather contour belt, and she'd subdued her hair as much as possible.

Logan couldn't help thinking that she still looked every inch the star. "We'll sit in the back of the church," he said, understanding her desire not to cause a commotion that would take anything away from Diane.

They waited until everyone was seated in the church before slipping into a back pew without being noticed. Music from the organ and a few string instruments filled the church and made Justine a little nervous. She'd never attended a formal wedding.

During high school her friends who married ran off to a justice of the peace across the state line in South Carolina. That's exactly what she and Brady did. She'd been underage, but no one had bothered to ask. She couldn't remember anything about the ceremony, except that the man who'd performed it had a stain on his tie, and his wife, who'd acted as witness, wore her hair in pink curlers. There'd been no pictures, no rice, not even a bridal bouquet. Afterward they'd joined the other members of the band and gone on to play a gig at a club in the next county. A few months later the instant fame they'd all been dreaming of caught up with them and Justine turned eighteen at about the same time. She'd always wished that they'd waited to get married later in a church filled with music and flowers.

All the weddings she'd attended after that, marriages of band members and friends of band members, the people she knew during the next few years, were wild events that had very little to do with the sacrament of marriage.

The moment the first strains of "Here Comes the Bride" filled the church and Diane started up the aisle on the arm of her ruddy-complexioned father, Justine started to cry. Logan saw the first tear make its way down her cheek, and he reached for her hand. Justine held on tightly through the ceremony that ended in a rush of excitement as Diane turned to retrieve her bouquet from her maid of honor and together she and Frank swept down the aisle. By then, Justine's face was wet with tears.

"Was I a total fool?" she asked, turning toward Logan as they inched through traffic on the way to the reception.

Logan shook his head. "Not at all," he said. "It was a beautiful ceremony." Then he admitted, "I felt like crying myself."

Justine looked at him, her eyes glistening with leftover tears as well as delight. "You almost cried?" she asked.

He nodded, and she reached out to hug him in happiness. "I'm so glad," she said. "That makes me love you even more."

Logan stopped at a red light. "Say that again."

"I'm so glad—"

"No, the last part," he insisted.

"It makes me like you even more."

"That's not what you said, Justine."

"I know." She looked away as the light changed and Logan drove the two remaining blocks to the hotel, turning into the enclosed parking lot. He was beginning to learn how to avoid the fans, but that wasn't the only reason for parking inside. As they drove into the darkened underground lot, he asked Justine, "What did you really say?"

"I love you, Logan," came the barely audible answer.

"Let's skip this reception and go to my apartment where we can be alone and I can tell you how much I love *you*, Justine."

She didn't even have a chance to answer. Although he'd parked at the far end of the garage, Diane and Frank found them. Horn blaring, streamers flying, they pulled up beside Logan's car.

"Come on, you two," Frank called out. "Let's head to the champagne and get this event inaugurated."

With a quick glance at each other, Justine and Logan let themselves be swept up in the festivities, which continued in one of the hotel's main ballrooms until almost midnight. Only once did Logan get Justine by herself again. That happened near the end of the evening when they found themselves in a semiquiet corner alone with the music. There Logan took Justine in his arms and swayed to the beat, holding her as close as he dared. "This is my idea of being out in the world," he said, "a big crowd where I can still have you all to myself."

"I know," Justine agreed. "I haven't even had to sign autographs except for the flower girls, and that was fun." She giggled as she'd done often that night, not from the champagne but from pure merriment. It had been years since Justine had been around so many people without being mobbed. "We're choosing wisely."

"Let's keep it up," he said. "We can live in the real world with the rest of the humans. We just have to be selective. It can work for us, my darling," he whispered against her ear.

"I know. I know." Her voice was once more close to tears. "Do you think it's all because of the wedding, all these feelings—the sadness, the happiness, the—"

"Love," Logan said, and again he felt it welling up inside, the feeling he knew was love. "Yes, the wedding had something to do with it but only because it reminded us of our own happiness. I do love you, Justine," he whispered again just as the orchestra sounded a drumroll to announce that Diane was about to throw her bouquet.

Justine didn't even have to reach for it. Diane threw it right to her.

Chapter Nine

Logan had hardly seen Justine in the four days since they'd been at La Quinta. The respite during which they'd belonged only to each other was over, just as they'd feared. She was performing again, and the stardom that was no part of Logan and that he wanted no part of surrounded her again.

It wasn't Justine's fault. It just happened. It was happening now as Logan watched her last full rehearsal before the opening. Justine had known he wanted to be at the rehearsal, and she'd insisted that she wanted him there, but Logan was at a table far in the back of the cabaret for a reason. He knew her feelings about closed rehearsals. She'd always used the excuse that the producers demanded them when it was actually Justine who made the demands. So Logan stayed out of the way.

In fact, the room was crowded with people, but they were a part of the staff, the retinue that accompanied Justine on singing dates. They usually brought her comfort, but today comfort was nowhere to be seen. For twenty minutes Justine and her director had been trying to explain their lighting complaints to Señor Ortego.

"But Señorita Justine," Ortego offered, "these are the very finest lighting systems. All from Los Angeles as I have told you."

"The main spots just aren't properly hung, Señor Ortego," Justine repeated as she'd done several times during the lighting rehearsal the day before, getting some changes but obviously not all.

"Did you have someone move that back light yet?" the director asked.

In fact, the light hadn't been moved, and so further time was taken to make the change with Señor Ortego rushing around, hoping to make professionals out of the amateur cabaret staff.

The band disassembled for a break, and Justine joined Logan at the table. "I'm going to let my director do the rest of the arguing," she said as she sank into a chair beside him. "Was I terrible?"

"Not at all. You've been very gracious considering all the problems. We've learned one thing from this experience. Professional equipment is no good without a professional staff to operate it."

Justine shook her head in frustration. "I know. We should have brought lighting people along, but that would really have increased the group, which is quite large enough, as you've observed."

Logan laughed and took her hand. "Oh, you mean your director, conductor, band members, hairdresser, costumer, makeup man, secretary, et cetera, et cetera?"

Justine joined in the laughter. "Yes, that's the group. I guess you and I haven't really had enough time together," she understated.

"Except in bed," he whispered, reminding her of the lazy hour they'd grabbed in their room that morning. Even that memory was interrupted by one of Justine's staff who had questions about seating for the celebrity guests. Logan stifled a yawn and released her hand.

"You still mind it, don't you?" she asked when they were alone again, and he knew what she was talking about.

"No," he tried, and then amended, "Yes, I do. I have a tough time when you're *on*. The wedding was fun, surrounded by friends. That was a good way to break out of our shell, but now here we are back with your groupies."

"It comes with the territory."

"Don't you get tired of it? Haven't you ever thought of just chucking it all away?" Logan had never asked her that question before, had only thought about it as he began to realize again when she stepped into the spotlight how all-encompassing this was for both of them.

Justine shook her head. "I've wanted this all my life. I've fought hard for it and could never just walk away. I *like* to stand out there in front of an audience and do what I do best. I thrive on that, Logan, and I could never give it up, even if I wanted to."

Sometimes she *did* want to give it all up, walk away from the pressure and the pain of performing. Although it had taken a toll on her, she still relished it and probably always would. "It's a part of me now. Remember that saying, 'the one who rides the tiger can never dismount'?" she asked, smiling ruefully. "I learned long ago that I was up there alone, couldn't get down and certainly couldn't depend on anyone but myself."

Those were sad words trying to be brave, Logan thought. He cupped her face in his hands. "I'm here, Justine. You can depend on me."

At that moment the director called out from the stage, "Justine, we're almost ready." She let a sigh escape, and it, too, seemed sad.

Logan's hand was still on her face, fingers lingering along the curve of her chin, reluctant to release her. "It's going well," he assured her, "except for the lights."

"Yes, except for the lights," she repeated.

"Don't give in until everything's the way you want it, Justine," he insisted. "Make them work until they get it right."

She smiled. "I'm not sure that can ever happen. If the back light is properly placed, I won't worry about the overhead."

"You don't have to open tomorrow. We can put it off until the lights are perfect. I'm serious, Justine. Change the overhead. Change anything."

"I'll see how it works now," she said, moving away and causing his fingers to drop from her face.

Logan was far from an expert in such matters but as the room darkened and the strategically placed lights slowly came up on Justine alone in the middle of the stage, he couldn't imagine a better effect. He felt a chill as he looked at her, and when the first notes of her song were released, slowly, almost agonizingly from her lips, the chill spread. If there was anything wrong with the lighting, it would never be noticed. Justine was radiant.

As she went through her numbers Logan thought of their time together and how close they'd become. He knew her so well, maybe as well as anyone would ever know Justine Hart. He knew her vulnerabilities, her fears. More importantly, he'd seen how hard she tried to keep them hidden. She accomplished that expertly, onstage and off. Only when they'd been on St. Cat's alone did she finally let her vulnerability show. Well, it certainly didn't show now. He was very proud of her.

Watching Justine perform, it was difficult for Logan to picture little Clara Johnson, insecure and afraid. He couldn't even picture her on the beach at St. Cat's admitting those fears. Neither version of Justine came into focus. For all else that she might have been or feared she would become again, Justine Hart was a star, and Logan reminded himself that she might never be able to lead an ordinary life, at least not the kind of life he led.

As he watched her and listened to her in that darkened room in which she lit every corner with her glow, hardly needing spotlights, he tried to think of himself fitting into her life. Once more the focus blurred. His image and Justine's couldn't seem to blend into one sharp, clear picture. Once he'd thought it would be easy. That had been before he found out what it was *really* like in Justine's world. Then he'd thought it would be difficult.

Now he wondered if it would even be possible. He'd thought so when they'd been holed up together at his apartment or hers. He'd even thought so at the wedding. Now the doubts were beginning to surface. As he watched her, he tried to put his fears down. Soon he succeeded and lost himself again in her performance.

An hour later, as she ended the rehearsal, Logan realized that he could have sat there and listened to her sing all day. But Justine and her director were satisfied that all of the problems were solved.

"At least if not solved, made less apparent," Justine told Logan late that afternoon when they broke away from her retinue and escaped for a walk alone on the beach, their first quiet time together outside the hotel room. Justine was wearing her "disguise," one which they'd concocted very carefully on the first day at La Quinta but which she'd never even had time to try out. Their main acquisition had been a floppy straw hat that made her look inconspicuous, just like any other tourist, and also covered her abundant red hair which she'd pulled back and tied with a ribbon. They'd added a pair of ordinary brown framed sunglasses, faded blue shorts, one of Logan's shirts and no shoes.

"I think it's the bare feet that keeps them away," Logan observed as they passed another couple, who didn't even glance in her direction. "Justine Hart has never been caught without her high heels."

"Even on the beach," she agreed. "I once played a resort in the south of France and walked along the beach after a press conference in red high-heeled sandals. It was a little ridiculous," she admitted.

"But the reporters liked it." It wasn't a question.

"Adored it," she said with a laugh.

As they walked among the long shadows of luxury hotels and condominiums that crowded the beach, Justine commented, "It's beautiful here but—"

"St. Cat's is better," Logan finished for her.

"I hope it never gets spoiled with luxury like all the other resorts," she said.

"As long as Carter has the only airport, I think we can be pretty certain that St. Cat's will stay just the way it is." Logan was thoughtfully silent before he added, "Let's go back for a few days after you finish the date here."

Justine started to object, thinking of the commitments she'd made in New York and then realizing that none of them was so important that Adele couldn't do some juggling and make everything work. "For New Year's!" she said excitedly.

"Carter would welcome us, I'm sure."

"Oh, Logan, let's call him now."

"No need to," Logan answered. "He'll be here tomorrow."

"For the opening? Why didn't you tell me?" she scolded.

"I wanted it to be a surprise, but obviously I'm no good at keeping secrets from you. Frank and Diane are coming down, too," he said, letting out the other secret.

"Logan, how marvelous!" She gave him an excited hug. "And your parents sent flowers."

"They're becoming big fans," Logan said. "As much as they'd seemed to miss me over the holidays, that's not the whole story. They would have been happy to add me to the other children and grandchildren gathered around the Christmas tree, but it was you they wanted to have up there."

"Do you really think so?"

He tightened his arm around her. "Of course. They like you, Justine. We all do—all the troupe that's following you here, not just your coterie but Carter and Diane and Frank."

"I know," she said wonderingly. "I can't believe they're coming."

Justine and Logan had walked well past the hotels and had almost reached the little cabana where they'd had a drink the day that seemed to Logan like centuries ago. It was twilight, and there were no other people left on the beach. He held her closer. "Well, it's going to be a tough assignment for Frank and Diane, leaving the New York streets full of slushy snow to walk on the beach and be pampered by the sun." Logan shook his head. "What a chore."

Justine laughed. "They don't *have* to come. Why, they're still almost honeymooners."

"Yes, I'm going to have to speak to Frank about all these vacations he's taking. Enough is enough," Logan said with a laugh.

"I guess he needs to come down and see how his clients' investments turned out," Justine suggested.

Logan stopped and took her by the shoulders. "Don't you understand, Justine, they're coming to see *you*. So is Carter." He reached out and took off her sunglasses. "That's why my parents sent the flowers."

"Well..." She still seemed doubtful.

Logan pulled off her hat, untied the ribbon and let her red hair fall free. "Believe me, Justine. They're here for *you*. That's also why I'm here, darling," he added.

They were all alone except for an attendant in the cabana, and he was dozing at the empty bar. Justine relaxed and let Logan hold her.

"Are you nervous?" he asked finally.

She nodded against his shoulder. "I'm always nervous before a show, but in many ways it's a good kind of nerves. It gets me going. I want them all to like me."

"They already like you, Justine," he told her again.

"I don't mean just my friends. I mean everyone in the audience. That's why I work so hard and give my best every time, so they'll like me and accept me."

"They always do," he assured her. "You know that."

"I suppose I do, but the real confidence doesn't come until I get up there on the stage and can feel that love. Then I'm sure of them. All of them except you, that is," she said in a voice that tried to be flippant.

"Hey," he said, stepping back to look down at her. "What are you talking about, Justine?"

"You like me," she said, "but not my life-style, not all the trappings that go with my being Justine."

Logan thought carefully about that before he answered. She'd moved away and begun walking down the beach. He caught up with her. "I don't dislike your life-style except when it takes you away from me. Which it's done a lot in the past four days," he added.

"I warned you, Logan."

He could only nod. She *had* warned him.

"The warnings weren't about what I expected so much as what I feared would happen. You thought it would all be so easy. I guess I did, too," she admitted. "Maybe that's why I kept running back to you no matter how determined I was to stay away, beginning on St. Cat's."

Logan walked silently beside her, and Justine talked on, as if to herself, about the way she'd vacillated. "I was determined to avoid you, but as quickly as I said to myself, *stay away*, I turned and fell into your arms."

"I remember when we first came to La Quinta," he said thoughtfully. "You were so aloof. Did you feel something for me then, Justine? Did you know what would happen between us?"

She shook her head. "I don't think so. Or maybe I did, deep down in my subconscious. The real reason I kept my distance was because I was determined not to mix my personal life with my business life."

"As it turned out, that hasn't been a problem between us," Logan said.

"No, it hasn't," she admitted. There'd been no conflict with Logan's firm handling her finances. Decisions, such as the one about La Quinta, had been discussed with Frank. As he'd promised, Logan hadn't interfered. "It's the part about me, who I am, that hasn't worked, has it, Logan?"

She stopped and looked up at him. Her hair was tangled around her face; a dozen freckles were scattered across her nose. He'd noticed them first in the sunlight of St. Cat's. They'd faded in New York, and now the sun had tempted them out again. She looked like a little girl. He had a sudden desire to hold her and protect her, but she was Justine. She stood alone, dependent on no one in spite of her vulnerability.

"We haven't given the rest of it time to work," he said.

"Do you think it ever will?"

"It's going to be difficult," Logan answered, voicing a concern he'd tried not to even let himself think about, "as long as you remain Justine."

She was looking away from him. With one bare foot she drew a line absently in the sand. He watched her foot move; she'd made the letter *J*.

"Do you want me to give it up, stop being Justine?" she asked.

He didn't know how to answer that. Their life-styles were so opposed. She was bound and determined to keep on being famous just as he was bound and determined to avoid fame at all costs. Yet his feelings for her were strong, and for so long—during those weeks in New York and right up to the time they got to La Quinta—he'd felt sure it could work. Then La Quinta happened and reminded him of the fame all over again. Maybe *he* just couldn't take it. Maybe it was his problem and he didn't have what was needed to conquer his jealousy.

With his bare foot Logan made the letter *L* next to the *J* in the sand. Then he formed a heart shape around the two letters just as he might have done as a teenager on the beach with his girlfriend. He smiled; she returned the smile, and he put his arms around her again. In less than twenty-four hours, Justine would be up on the stage, and he would be in the audience, proud. Justine needed to be sure of his pride in her.

"I don't want you to give up anything you want for yourself," he said softly. "I'll be there tomorrow when you knock 'em dead, and I'll be applauding louder than anyone."

That only answered the question of tomorrow, not of the next day and the next and all the days of their lives—separately or apart—to come.

Logan awoke early the morning of Justine's opening, quietly got up and dressed, knowing Justine needed her sleep before the show, also knowing that as soon as she woke up she'd be surrounded by her helpers and be on her way to the cabaret. He wouldn't see her again that day, and so he decided to get out quickly before the members of her retinue began to arrive and whisk her away. He called the desk and asked them to ring her at nine o'clock. Then with only a brief glance at Justine cozily curled up in the sheets, Logan scribbled a quick note and silently left the room.

Two hours later, the telephone wake-up call jarred Justine out of what had not been the peaceful sleep Logan imagined. She'd been plagued by intermittent dreams about the show in which everything that could go wrong, went wrong. The nerves weren't unusual for Justine, but the dreams were. She got out of bed a little troubled, and when her secretary arrived half an hour later, she was still thinking about the dreams.

And she missed Logan. His note had been sweet but somehow not quite enough: "This is your day so I'll leave you to your preparations, but I'll be there tonight when you bring down the house." In those words there was something unsaid that corresponded

to the breach between them. Yet he'd been right to
leave, Justine realized. As much as she needed him
emotionally, right now and up until show time were
the hours of last-minute details, and only she could
deal with them.

So the independent, confident Justine went into
action. Not until minutes before going on stage did she
think again of the dreams and experience again the
nerves, and then the nerves were worse than ever before. They overcame her as the makeup man applied
final touches, the dresser made an extra tuck and the
hairstylist tried to tame a recalcitrant curl.

He failed, stood back and observed the overall look
and declared, "Wild is best, Justine. It suits you. Let's
not do another thing."

Justine took a deep breath and tried to replace the
nerves with a little patter. "I've been telling you that
for years, Charlie."

"I'm a slow study," came the response. With a kiss
on her cheek, he added, "Break a leg, baby," saw her
suddenly pale face and observed, "The nerves are
worse than usual, aren't they?"

"Umm," Justine admitted as her stomach seemed
to head upward toward her throat.

"Good. That means you'll be *better* than ever." He
paused and cocked his head. "There it is, your final
call. Want me to go up with you?"

"No, thanks, Charlie," Justine declined as the
hairdresser flicked his comb one last time and she
headed up the wrought-iron steps to the stage.

* * *

Logan's table was the best in the cabaret. Many celebrities had flown down for the opening, but the people who really mattered were at his table. Carter, Frank and Diane, Adele. Logan had also included in his party the enthusiastic and ever-smiling Señor Ortego who, all the problems having been solved to everyone's satisfaction, couldn't stop looking around at the celebrity-studded crowd.

"So many people, so many stars," he said to Logan, his handsome face beaming. "All here at my cabaret!"

Logan couldn't suppress a smile. Señor Ortego had taken his publicity work so seriously that Cabaret La Quinta was not just his job but his club.

"And just to think, Mr. Addison," he continued, "the famous Justine opening our holiday show! I could not have hoped for better. You have seen the Christmas lights outside on the palm trees? That was a good idea, I think, to lend an even more festive mood and to give our guests the Christmas spirit."

"Yes," Logan agreed, "a very good idea."

Sitting back, Señor Ortego sipped his glass of celebration champagne and turned to share his excitement with Adele.

Ortego's wasn't the only pleased face. Frank Norwood was a happy bridegroom *and* a happy investment manager. This was turning out to be one of Norwood and Addison's best ventures. "We were already heading for the black before Justine, but now," he said to Logan, "we're in clover. On top of that, you and Justine, like me and Diane..." He gave his new wife a hug, and his face lit up.

"Frank's gotten downright lovey-dovey since he became a married man," Diane said with a smile. Logan couldn't help but observe that she, too, seemed more romantic. She'd shed a little of her brisk and businesslike persona and softened noticeably. Not that Diane wasn't still an advertising executive par excellence; she'd always be that. But there was a glow now that hadn't been there before, the same glow that Logan had observed on Frank's face since the wedding. Somehow it gave him an ache of jealousy.

Carter's arrival added another beaming face to the group and eliminated Logan's momentary depression. He saw the dapper figure approach from across the floor and rose to greet him.

"Carter. Over here. Glad you could make it."

Carter reached for Logan's outstretched hand. "We had some problems before takeoff and just landed a few minutes ago. For a while there, I was afraid I would miss Justine's opening, which would never do," he declared.

Logan introduced Carter to the others at the table. "You look none the worse for wear," Logan said as he offered Carter a seat beside him.

Carter brushed perfunctorily at the front of his dinner suit and adjusted his tie. "A little dust here and there, perhaps, but all in one piece."

Carter was considerably more than *in one piece*. His tuxedo was wrinkle free, the shirtfront gleaming as white as his perfectly combed hair. His patent leather shoes reflected the candlelight on the table as he crossed one leg over the other.

Obviously, everyone at the table was duly impressed with the appearance among them of the worldly Carter Graham, but his interest for the moment was clearly in Logan.

"I can't tell you how glad I was to learn that you would be here with Justine for the opening. When I left you two in New York, I wasn't at all sure what I would find when next we met."

"I don't think Justine and I are quite sure, either," Logan answered honestly.

"These things often take time—and work. A lot of work on both your parts. When two people want to be together and yet don't seem to belong, then they simply have to try harder than others to overcome the differences. It can be done," Carter added firmly.

Logan didn't answer because he wasn't sure whether, as Carter suggested, the differences could be overcome, and talking about her brought on all the doubts and uncertainties that had plagued him for the past four days.

Seeing her was another matter, and now he was about to see her again—for the first time since he'd left her bed that morning.

The lights had dimmed, and the audience had become suddenly, almost magically, quiet. There was no more conversation, no clinking of glasses, hardly a breath drawn as a voice announced simply from the darkness, "Ladies and gentlemen, Justine!"

The band began its introduction before the spotlight came up on her, and during that time Logan felt a shared tension with Justine. Even in the darkness, he knew exactly how she looked at that moment. He could feel her tremble, and his heart pounded in what he knew was the exact racing rhythm of her own.

When the light hit her and she sounded the first soft note of the first song, both she and Logan relaxed. But the audience didn't relax. They went wild, drowning out the voice, drowning out even the band as they recognized the song, her most famous one, which she'd first sung for Logan on St. Cat's. It had become their song, but as far as the audience was concerned "Our Song Unending" belonged to *them*, and the applause continued for so long that the band finally gave up, its members sitting back and waiting, instruments silent.

She was wearing a black shimmering sequined dress, less wild and far-out than her fans were used to but more suited to this club and this crowd. Her hair was a bright flame that danced in the light, her brown eyes flashed and her wide smile enticed. Logan forgot everything that had troubled him during the day, everything from all the days they'd been at La Quinta.

He was a part of Justine, the sensational woman on the stage, singing now to a hushed crowd. She was *something*, a real star, and she was his Justine, the woman he held in the night and made love to. He joined the applause that ended the first song and led into the next, all his senses filled with her.

Halfway through the show, she stopped to say a few words to the audience, to greet those she knew and welcome them all to the Christmas season at Cabaret La Quinta. Her voice was soft and throaty, that voice he'd been entranced with from the first time he heard her speak, was still entranced with. When she smiled and caught his eye, Logan realized that this was the woman he loved. When she broke into her next song he realized, his head pounding from the applause, that he could never really have her.

She belonged to *them*, to her fans. The little problems he'd been bothered by in the past few days weren't really what it was all about. With a sudden blinding flash of insight, Logan saw clearly that this love, the audience's love, was what separated them, and she could never give it up for his love. He watched the rest of her spectacular show with a sense of pride that was mixed with foreboding. She couldn't want him when she had all this.

The last number, as it turned out, was far from her last. The audience wouldn't let her leave. Finally, Justine declared in a hoarse voice that she had only one song left in her, but it would be a rousing one, a wild rock number that she'd first sung very early in her career and that her audience remembered well.

The lights dimmed and then went up bright, all of them hitting her with full force, red, yellow and orange gels crazily dancing on her. She'd just stepped forward under the overhead light when Logan noticed a shimmering effect that he hadn't remembered from the rehearsal of her encores. A light somewhere wasn't steady. Somewhere... He looked up just as the overhead lamp broke loose from the scaffolding and crashed toward her.

"Move, Justine, move," he screamed out, but it was already too late. She'd looked up, too, knowing something was wrong, just as the heavy glass and steel lamp hit her.

Logan could only thank God that she'd been unconscious during the two horrible hours that followed. They'd driven through the night to the airport, flown to Miami in Carter's plane as a doctor who'd been in the audience stopped the bleeding, wrapped her head in a makeshift bandage and gave her a shot in case she regained consciousness.

That hadn't happened until they reached the hospital in Miami, until she was on a stretcher held by two orderlies who raced down the hall toward the emergency room with Logan by her side, holding her hand.

Carter had stayed behind in the office to fill out the forms, advising the admitting nurse, curtly, "She has no family. I'll sign everything. I'm her uncle," he lied, "and she needs immediate attention."

Justine felt the pain before she opened her eyes. It pounded on one side of her head she thought, but she couldn't tell which side. She tried to reach up and find the pain with her hand, but she couldn't move. Did that mean she was paralyzed? She tried to cry out, ask someone, but the words wouldn't come. Justine knew she should open her eyes and yet she was afraid of what she might see so she kept them tightly shut and tried again to speak. Nothing. Still nothing.

She was lying flat, but she was moving. All around she heard the mingled sounds of feet running and voices whispering. Finally she forced her eyes open. Above, the white ceiling flashed by; to the sides, white walls flashed by; bending over her was a white-clad figure holding a bottle. There was a tube hanging from it. She followed the tube with her eyes down to her arm. There it ended. It was an IV, and it was inserted into her vein.

Justine had felt all that, seen all that through the pain. Still she couldn't speak, couldn't ask what or why or how. Then she suddenly remembered. The light, the big overhead that she'd argued with Señor Ortego about had crashed to the floor but not before striking her—in the face!

She tried again to move and succeeded in lifting her arm slightly. "Don't," a voice said. She saw a dark face bend down, readjust the IV and advise, "Try not to move."

They'd stopped running. The white walls were farther away. They were in a room, a big room, and overhead there was another light. "No!" she screamed out as she imagined the light falling toward her.

"Justine." A voice spoke. A hand reached out and touched her shoulder. "It's all right." It was Logan's voice, but he was on the other side. She couldn't see him, couldn't turn her head.

"Logan."

"Don't worry," he assured her. "You're in the hospital in Miami. Everything's going to be all right."

The sound that came from her lips was a cry that was filled with agony. It tore at his heart. He held her hand and assured her again, "You'll have the best doctors, Justine. It *is* going to be all right. Just believe me, please."

"Mr. Addison, you'll need to leave now," a nurse advised. "We're going to prepare her for surgery."

Logan heard Justine's cry again. He bent closer so she could feel his lips on her cheek. "Hang in there, Justine," he said. "I love you."

Chapter Ten

Logan looked out of the window of Frank Norwood's office into the bleakness of New York in late February. It was no bleaker than his own wintery mood. "I don't know what to do about her," he confided to Frank.

"She'll be all right when all this is over and she can get back to work," Frank said. He put away the portfolio he'd been reviewing when Logan had come into his office. Logan saw him shift the papers quickly as if they were of no importance, and he sensed that Frank was hoping for a heart-to-heart talk, the one Logan had been skirting for almost two months since Justine's accident. Frank hadn't been insistent, only concerned. Diane *had* been insistent. Whenever the three of them had dined together, she'd tried to get

Logan to open up about Justine, but he hadn't been able to. Until now.

"Sit down, Logan," Frank advised. "Your pacing is making me nervous."

"Sorry," Logan said, still not giving up the pacing to light in one place.

"I'm amazed that you've gotten so much work done these past two months the way you're fretting."

Logan slowed down and, finally, stopped, leaning against the ledge beneath Frank's panoramic window. "Nervous energy kept me going. In fact, I think I've done better work recently because I've been throwing myself into my client's problems to forget mine." Logan took off his glasses and put them on top of his head. "I don't know why I'm saying *my* problems. I mean Justine's."

"They're yours, too, Logan. She's unsettled, and you're the one who's getting the ulcer. Be patient. It'll all work out."

Logan almost laughed, but there was no humor in the sound that caught on his lips. "That's what I used to say to Justine about us, about our relationship. 'It will all work out,' I told her frequently." Logan finally gave in to Frank's demanding stare and crossed the room to sit in a chair opposite the desk. "I'm not even sure what I meant except that she'd decide to give up her career and be what I wanted her to be. The unspoken message was: you'll see how wonderful it is to be the woman loved by Logan Addison and nothing more. What a fool I was."

"At least you've found that out."

"Too late," Logan said. "Now she doesn't want her career, and she doesn't want me, either. I'm damned if I know what she wants."

"Logan, she's a fabulous star who had a terrible accident, and she's having trouble fighting back from it. That's not unusual. After all, she broke eighteen bones in that beautiful face. Lord, I didn't even know there *were* eighteen bones in a person's face."

"The damage was extensive," Logan commented, "and she thinks she'll never heal, that the scars will be there forever."

"She may be right. Plastic surgery is good but it still can't work miracles."

Logan disagreed. "In her case, the doctors feel sure it'll be completely successful. She has two more operations to go. One this week and then the last one in six months. After that, she'll be almost like new. Any differences will be obvious only to her. I'm pretty sure she realizes that and is just using the scars as an excuse."

"For what?" Frank asked.

"I don't know, Frank. This last trip... Well, as far as she's concerned, it was the final trip."

A deep frown creased Frank's brow. "What happened?"

"I can't really pinpoint the problem. It all began with a damned milk shake."

Frank laughed and shook his head. "Tell me."

The story Logan related was one that he'd gone over a dozen times in his mind since returning from his latest visit to Justine, and he'd go over it again before he went to sleep that night, he had no doubt.

It had all begun with a silly argument that was nothing but meaningless words, but they were at least *words*, about her, about the two of them. On all of his earlier visits since the accident she'd talked to him without really talking, as if they were strangers again, on guard should they get too close. Well, they'd gotten close that time, but Logan couldn't claim anything had come of it.

He'd flown out to be with her in Palm Springs where she was recuperating. In the beginning he'd been with her every day, every hour—at her side in the Miami hospital, through the first surgery, through Christmas and then New Year's. He'd flown to Los Angeles with her for consultations with the specialists and he'd gone back again for the surgery.

The weeks had turned into a month and then another, and he'd flown back and forth between his work in New York and the condo she'd rented in Palm Springs. Yet she'd remained alone, even when he was there. Logan knew he should have felt pleased just to be with her. Except for the nurse, a stranger whom Justine kept a stranger, he was the only one she saw during those two months, but their closeness hadn't been anything like the closeness that Logan had known with Justine before. They couldn't be called strangers because he was *there*, with her, when no one else had that privilege, but it wasn't the same. Through it all he'd held back and let her set the mood. Until the last weekend.

She'd been out by the pool when Logan arrived. He saw her through the glass doors in the living room of her apartment. Because of the surgery, her skin was susceptible to the sun, and she had to wear a hat, the old straw hat from her disguise on La Quinta. To further insure that the sun's rays didn't reach her skin, she sat under a huge umbrella.

"How long has she been out there?" he asked the nurse.

He was told that Justine had been outside all morning, not moving from the chaise except when she periodically got up and cooled off in the shallow end of the pool. Logan took the drink the nurse had concocted for Justine and stepped through the sliding doors.

He stood for a moment on the edge of the patio and looked across toward the pool. The setting was idyllic. A bright sun shone in a cerulean-blue sky, but a slight breeze kept the air from being uncomfortably hot. The umbrella Justine sat beneath was a bright red and yellow. The chaise was a vivid blue, and so was her bikini. Two months ago, before the accident, Logan would have stepped into the colorful scene and into her arms. Anyone watching from the distance and not knowing the people involved would have expected him to do so now.

He didn't. Experience of the past weeks had cautioned him to avoid intimacy. He crossed to her, and she looked up with a slight smile and said, "Hello, Logan."

He put the frosty glass on the table beside her and brushed her arm with his hand, the only touch he dared. "This is a special milk shake that your nurse just blended. She wants you to try it."

"That is, *you* want me to try it."

Logan stifled a sigh and sat down on a patio chair beside her. "I think you're much too thin, Justine. Even when I looked out from the house, I could tell that you still hadn't gained any weight since the last time I was here. In fact, it looks like you've lost a couple of pounds." He picked up the glass and attempted to hand it to her. "This kind of high calorie drink will really help with—"

"Please, Logan," Justine interrupted, ignoring the proffered glass.

"If you just—"

"No," she said in a tone that wasn't unpleasant but was definitely final. "My weight is fine. I eat and drink what interests me, and that milk shake does not interest me in the slightest. She's made them before, and if you don't believe how bad they are, please feel free to taste it for yourself."

Not about to give up, Logan took a taste of the milk shake. He couldn't defend it at all. "I'll tell you what," he suggested. "I'll drive out the highway to that stand with the date shakes. They're the best anywhere or so I'm told, and they'll probably be just as good for you as this."

"Logan," Justine said, whipping off her glasses and looking at him straight in the eye. "Please stop fussing over me. My face may be scarred, but I'm not an invalid. If I want a date shake I can drive out to the Oasis myself. I'm not the slightest bit hungry or thirsty right now, thanks."

She put on her glasses, pulled her hat down a little farther and leaned back in the chaise. Realizing that this was the first time Logan had seen her since the bandages came off after the last surgery, Justine felt suddenly naked. She imagined that he was staring right at the swelling in her face and the scar that remained on her cheek. She put her hand on her cheek to hide what she'd come to think of as her deformity and wished he would just go away. She'd been alone all week except for the nurse, and she wanted to keep on being alone. She didn't want to talk, much less think, and Logan's presence seemed to force her to do both. He reminded her of the past and the future, but as far as Justine was concerned, the past was a closed book and the future didn't exist.

Yet Justine realized she had no right to act so cross when Logan had come all this way to be with her and was trying to help. "I'm sorry," she said softly. "I didn't mean to be so short-tempered, Logan."

"Apology accepted." Her anger didn't bother him—in fact, he welcomed it. It was better than silence and forced politeness, both of which he'd had enough of in the past two months. "How are you feeling?" he asked.

"Depressed," she admitted, "and a little guilty that I'm the cause of so much unpleasantness in your life."

"In *my* life?" he asked, surprised.

"Yes, spending Christmas in the hospital in Miami, New Year's in the hospital in Los Angeles and almost every weekend watching me 'recover,'" she said, sounding the last word a little sarcastically.

"And being happy to see that recovery," he answered, giving another emphasis to the word, aware that Justine still didn't think her recovery would be complete and ready to hear her talk about it.

She didn't respond to his challenge. "What kind of life can this be for you, waiting from surgery to surgery? I'm certainly tired of it. I'm sure you are, too, and there's no end in sight.''

"Of course there is," he disagreed. "One more operation next week, the last one in this series and the least painful, according to the doctor. After that you should be nearly perfect."

Justine fingered her scar and shook her head in disagreement.

"Well, there may still be a slight scar," Logan admitted, "but it'll fade in time, and after the final surgery in the fall, it'll *all* be over."

"Yes," she said with a tone that continued the sarcasm.

"Justine, this kind of attitude isn't like you."

"Maybe *I'm* not like me," she flashed out at him.

Confused at that outburst, Logan backed away a little. "You'll look fine by Thanksgiving, and if there is any trace of imperfection, it can be hidden with makeup."

She gave an almost bitter laugh. "So long as I'm in my Justine image, everything will be fine, but what if I want to be Clara Johnson without the stage make-up?"

"Fine," Logan said. Once, that was just the image Logan would have liked. "I'll love you no matter who you want to be."

The pause that followed was long and seemed as if it would never end. In the silence, he remembered it all again and knew that she was remembering, too, the long days in the hospital when she'd lain there so still and white, tubes in her arms, her face bandaged. His heart had gone out to her then. He'd felt tender toward her and frightened for her and very, very worried. She hadn't responded at all. She'd just lain there, accepting. Then when they'd been together in Palm Springs during her recovery and between operations, the same bitter acceptance of what had happened and the same attitude toward Logan had existed.

When he'd held her she'd seemed so fragile that all he could think about was how much he'd loved her— and how he'd almost lost her. Her fragility as much as her unresponsiveness had kept them from being lovers during that time. He wouldn't have minded that if only they could have regained something of the other kind of closeness that had once existed between them.

He'd felt frustrated, helpless, almost frozen then. Now at least she was talking, but what she had to say next jolted him.

"Logan, I really think you should go back to New York tomorrow."

"What? I just got here, Justine."

"My surgery isn't until Wednesday, and it seems pointless for you to be away from your office that long. Frank is probably—"

"To hell with Frank," Logan said, surprising both Justine and himself with his anger. "I don't care about anything right now but you."

"That's the problem," Justine said, and then he heard what he hadn't expected. He'd wanted her to talk to him, but he hadn't wanted to hear this. "You're smothering me with your care and concern," she told him.

Logan had been in the act of reaching out to touch her arm when she said that. He drew back his hand and then quizzically rubbed his clenched jaw as he looked at her, trying to see something in her eyes besides the words she'd spoken. "I haven't meant to be overbearing, Justine."

"You make me feel more like a helpless outcast than I am."

"You're not an outcast," he shot back, the hurt giving way to irritation.

"Yes, I am," she retorted.

"Only because that's the way you want it," he challenged.

"All right. Maybe it is, but I don't need your pity and your...guilt."

Again her words startled him. After the weeks of near-silence, she was finally saying everything that she'd been holding back. "All right," he admitted. "I do feel some guilt, not just for introducing you to La Quinta in the first place but also for not insisting that a professional crew be hired to work the lights."

"I knew you'd been thinking about that," she said, almost triumphantly, before reminding him of the facts. "The choice to go to La Quinta was mine, not yours. As for the lights, you told me to make sure they were the way I wanted them. I did. That was my choice, too. I don't blame you, Logan, and I certainly don't want your pity."

"I don't pity you, Justine. Maybe," he added softly, "you pity yourself."

Justine stood up, adjusting her hat more firmly over her forehead, and started toward the house. "I think I'll drive out and get that milk shake."

"I'll come with you," he said.

"No, Logan—"

"Please." He'd gone after her and caught her by the arm. "We've started this talk, and I want to finish it.

I want to know how you're feeling. I want you to know how *I'm* feeling. We've been protecting each other too long. So do you want to drive or shall I?'' he asked, not letting her get away without him.

She shrugged, and he followed her through the house and out the back door. ''I'll drive,'' he said, leading her to his rented car.

Not until they got out on the highway did she speak, and her words were defensive. ''You don't know how I feel,'' she challenged. ''You don't know what's going on inside of me.''

''Then tell me, Justine,'' he urged.

''I have no idea what it'll be like, my future. I don't know what will happen to me.''

''We can work it out together.''

''No, this is my problem. I have to find the answers alone, Logan.''

Rather stiffly, he responded. ''I don't want to intrude in your life. I know how upset you've been—''

''That's it,'' she said quickly. ''That's what I can't bear, the condescension and the patronizing. I don't think you understand what I've been going through.''

''Yes, I do, Justine,'' he answered curtly, ''and that's what *I* can't bear, the hiding, the self-pity, the denial of your feelings about me.'' He turned off the highway where a huge sign announced, World Famous Oasis Shakes. He pulled up under the trees in the shade and turned off the engine. ''You're denying everything between us, Justine. You're denying that you love me.''

When she still didn't answer, he got out of the car, opened her door, and they walked toward the little stand. She started to go with him and then changed her mind. There was a picnic table under the palm trees. "I'll wait over there," she said. He knew that the kids behind the counter were just two more strangers she didn't have the courage to face, but he let her go.

When he brought the shakes to the table and sat down beside her, Logan spoke quietly without anything in his voice that she could call condescension. "I understand how you feel, Justine, but I want to be with you through all this. I think it's the time for us, for you and me. When the operation is over and you go back home to New York, we can get married and face the future together." He'd tried to slip the casual proposal of marriage into the conversation as if it were just another suggestion, but she responded quickly.

"Get married?" She was startled.

"Yes, Justine. I love you and you love me. Now more than ever, we should be together."

Justine shook her head so slowly that Logan felt tears sting at his eyes, tears over the sadness in her gesture, which was as confusing as it was disturbing.

"No," she said in a flat, emotionless voice. "Now, of all times, would be wrong for us. I'm tired, Logan, and I'm very unsure about everything. I'm going to have to be by myself. Please," she pleaded, "go back to New York and give me a chance to breathe."

Spoken there under the palm trees on a desolate, hot highway outside of Palm Springs, her words had the ring of finality in them.

That feeling of termination followed Logan back to New York. It was still with him when he finally talked to Frank. Even after talking, he couldn't shed the feeling.

* * *

"You look lovely," Adele said as she breezed into Justine's apartment two weeks later. "I'm so glad to have you back." She leaned over and kissed Justine's cheek. "Yes," she said, looking closer, "Sensational. Do I have plans!"

"Wait a minute, Adele," Justine said, holding up her hands. "Let's not talk about your plans yet. I look terrible and you know it. My face is still puffy, there's an indentation under my cheekbone and the scar is still visible."

"After the last surgery in the fall, everything will be back in shape. Until then, a little stage makeup—"

"I'm not ready to go back on stage. I don't look good enough."

Adele passed by Justine and headed toward the living room, sitting down on the art deco sofa. "That doesn't sound like you, Justine. You'll look a little different, that's all, and you always *were* different. But you were never vain."

"I know that," Justine admitted.

"I thought you did. Then what is it? What's the matter?"

Justine sat down beside Adele. It was good to have her here. She hadn't wanted company, but now she realized how much she'd missed the companionship of another person since Logan left her in Palm Springs. "I'm scared," she admitted. "The whole experience has been such a hideous trauma. When I close my eyes all I can remember is being on the stage and seeing the lamp fall and then waking up to the pain. I'm scared, Adele," she said in a voice that quivered and then broke down completely as she started to cry.

Adele enclosed her in an understanding hug. "I know how you feel," she said, "and maybe you're right. Maybe it's a little too soon to think about returning to the stage, but you need to get back into life, be around people."

"I don't want to," Justine said through her tears. "I don't want to be around anyone yet, even friends. I'm not sure I'll ever want to again."

"That's ridiculous, you'll get over it in time. I'll help you, and so will Logan."

Justine brushed at her eyes and looked through the tears at Adele. "I told him I didn't want to see him again."

"What? Did you mean *ever*?"

"I don't know what I meant."

"Do you love him?" Adele asked.

Justine nodded.

"And does he love you?"

"Yes; that is, I think so. He asked me to marry him." There was a quiver in Justine's voice that she tried to hide.

"Then obviously, he loves you."

"I'm not sure." Justine touched her hand to her face. It was an automatic gesture by now and had nothing to do with what she was feeling. She'd finally realized that. The scar was her excuse, and she was hiding behind it because she couldn't make any real decisions. After all the time she'd had to think, all she wanted was more time to think. And thinking so far had gotten her nowhere. "I sent him away," she told Adele. "I said terrible things to him, accused him of asking me to marry him only out of pity."

"I'm sure that's not true, Justine. It doesn't sound like Logan at all."

"No, it doesn't," Justine admitted. "I really don't have any doubts about his love. All my doubts are about myself." Justine leaned back against the sofa with an exhausted sigh but no more tears.

Adele lit a cigarette, got up and rummaged around looking for an ashtray. "I think there's one in the desk drawer," Justine said.

Adele found it and sat back down. "Now tell me about the doubts, Justine."

"Nothing has really worked for us from the day we came back from St. Cat's. No matter what happens, good or bad, everything just seems to get worse with Logan and me."

"Did you ever think of relaxing and giving it a chance? These things take time."

Justine found herself smiling. "That sounds just like Carter. He was happily married for thirty years so I guess he speaks from experience, but Adele—"

Adele interrupted with her throaty laugh. "I know, since my experience consists of a long line of unsuccessful marriages, who am I to give advice? Well, let's just say I didn't do what I'm advising you to do and look where it got me!"

Justine shook her head. "I told Logan that I needed to be alone. He left but still nothing's solved, and I'm still unsure. There was once a conflict between my feelings for him and for my fans. At least Logan thought it was a conflict. Now I'm afraid I'm going to lose him *and* my fans. I'm afraid...well, I'm just plain afraid."

"You can get whatever you want, Justine," Adele assured her. "You've always had a lucky star."

"That's the problem. I've always gotten what I wanted in the past. Now I'm not sure *what* I want. I know that I'm not ready to see Logan yet, even though I miss him. Lord, I miss him terribly, but I still feel a need for more time by myself."

"Hmm. New York isn't quite the place to fill that particular need, my dear. Not for you, anyway. Everybody's here. They've all been calling, and I don't know how much longer I'm going to be able to keep them away from your doorstep. I've canceled everything I can cancel, but pretty soon I'm going to be forced into some rescheduling for you."

"Not yet, Adele. Don't do anything yet."

Adele put out her cigarette and lit another one. "I should be getting back, but I dread going into that office with all those phones ringing off the hooks, especially when I have no answers." She turned to Justine. "I'll need a real firm decision soon."

"I'm going to St. Cat's," came the response.

"Why, may I ask?"

"To think."

Adele shook her head. "Honey, I don't want to sound preachy, but how much thinking can a person do? Maybe you need a little direction, Justine. Not from me, Lord knows. I'm no good at the psychological stuff, but maybe if you talked to someone who could help you get back on track."

"I've considered that, Adele, but I believe I can work it out by myself, in a place that feels comfortable to me. St. Cat's is that place."

"Well, you could be right. Carter Graham is a pretty understanding man." She stood up and reached for her bag. "Meanwhile, I'll get back to the telephones, try to stall them, and wait to hear from you."

Savoy's Revenge was just what Justine needed. For two days she lazed around the house, delighting in its old-world architecture, roaming from room to room under the breeze of indolently turning fans amid the wicker and chintz.

"I feel like I'm in a wonderful old hotel in the depths of safari country."

Carter laughed. "As well you should. Savoy's Revenge is a compilation of some of my favorite hotels in Africa and the Middle East. It was marvelous fun, achieving this mood."

Justine had reveled in it for two days and then she'd taken Carter's Jeep and explored the rest of the island, avoiding the lagoon where she and Logan had first made love. But she hadn't been able to avoid Logan. He filled her mind more and more, taking over every time she tried to concentrate on her future.

"Maybe he *is* your future," Carter told her at dinner after she'd returned from her roaming, taken a cool bath in the footed tub in her room and put on a long gauzy white dress to join him in the dining room.

As usual, Carter was dressed for dinner in a tuxedo. He picked up his shrimp fork, speared a shrimp from the iced bowl before him and asked, "Did you ever think about it—that Logan's your future?"

"I think of it all the time."

"Good." Carter didn't say anything more on the subject. That had been his pattern during the time she'd been with him, to listen, comment succinctly and then go on to another subject. He'd dealt with all her problems over their meals together—the accident, the surgery, the scars, her career, Logan—letting Justine pour out her feelings, and only occasionally giving advice. The advice was always in the form of a suggestion such as the one tonight, for her to mull over.

She did so, aloud, weighing pros and cons and voicing her fears not just about her future and whether there was a place for Logan in it, but about Logan's feelings and whether he really wanted to be a permanent part of her life.

"He said that's what he wanted," Carter reminded her.

"That was during the depths of my depression between operations. He was reacting, Carter. Under those circumstances he wasn't necessarily expressing his real feelings."

Carter thought that over as he consumed another shrimp. "Well, you aren't depressed anymore," he observed. "I believe Justine is back, as I knew she would be. So maybe it's time you consulted him again," came the second suggestion of the evening.

"Maybe," Justine echoed.

"In the meantime, how would you like to go to London with me for a few days?"

Justine waited for a servant to clear away her cocktail dish and then asked, "Are you talking about some time soon?"

"I'm talking about the day after tomorrow."

Justine's eyebrows shot up.

"There's going to be a revival of one of the most drawing room of my drawing room comedies in the

West End next month, and I just can't resist going over to see a few rehearsals to make sure they're getting it all right." He chuckled. "I never was able to keep out of the way."

Justine laughed. "I know they look forward to having you there."

"I suppose they do, now that I'm in my dotage. In the old days, of course, I was far less subdued. So, what do you say? Want to go with me?"

"I don't know, Carter."

Carter moved the centerpiece of tropical flowers so he could get an unobstructed view of Justine. "I think it might be good for you. Of course, I can't promise anything in the way of weather. It's a damnable climate this time of year—all times of year, in fact. Rain, fog, the typical London complaints, but you know all about them. You've played London many times."

"Yes, I have," Justine said, remembering the mass hysteria of the crowds of British kids at her shows. They'd always been among her best audiences. "I'm not sure I'm ready for crowds yet, Carter."

"Well, there will be crowds, no doubt about it. You're familiar to Londoners, and so am I, even after all these years. I certainly can't promise you privacy. But you'll have to face them again sometime, Justine."

"I know that, but I'm not quite ready yet."

Carter looked across at her with steady bright blue eyes and asked, "What are you ready for?"

"Logan," she said softly.

He smiled. "Time to test the water, face up to your fears?"

"I think so. Could I catch a ride with you as far as New York?"

"I have a better idea." Carter was suddenly very cheerful, which Justine knew was on account of her desire to see Logan again. He hadn't tried to push her in that direction since she'd been at Savoy's Revenge, but he'd let her talk about Logan, encouraged her to talk about him and get in touch with her feelings. He'd succeeded.

"Why don't you stay here at Savoy's Revenge? When I get to New York, I'll call Logan. I have a feeling he'll jump at the idea of a few days on St. Cat's—the two of you, alone, with no old curmudgeon to get in the way. I expect he'll like that very much."

"I hope so," Justine said, all of a sudden unsure again, aching to see him but afraid for them both.

Chapter Eleven

Angelique came running across the wide lawn, scattering a flock of colorful birds in her wake as she shouted for Justine.

"M'selle, M'selle," she called, her steps a rapid dance, her sandaled feet barely touching the grass.

Justine knew what the excitement was all about. She went down the hall and stepped out on the wide veranda just as Angelique reached the bottom of the stairs.

"Ils sont là," Angelique said, pointing to the sky. "Ils sont là."

Justine returned the smile and tried not to show her nerves. She knew enough French to understand that Logan had arrived, not only Logan but Steve, as well, the real object of Angelique's enthusiastic cries. With some sort of déjà vu in mind, Logan had made sure that he chartered Steve's plane for his return to St. Cat's.

Hearing the excitement, the houseboy had already headed across the lawn toward the Jeep. Angelique looked after him longingly and then turned to pout in Justine's direction.

"All right," Justine said, "go meet the plane."

"Attends, je viens," Angelique called out to the driver of the Jeep. He turned the vehicle around and waited for her to hop in beside him before heading for the airstrip to pick up Steve and Logan.

Justine, feeling a sort of jealousy at Angelique's bright-eyed anticipation, turned and went back into the coolness of the house. It wouldn't take long for them to reach the airfield, load the luggage and return to the house, and Justine, devoid of Angelique's assurance about herself and her relationship, wished that she could stretch out the minutes. She needed time to build up her confidence.

She walked down the long hall, missing Carter. He'd reached her the day before on Martin's radio, calling to say that rehearsals weren't what they used to be, none of the strife and strain and marvelous temper tantrums. That observance wasn't the real reason he'd gone to the trouble to contact her. He'd called because he wanted to find out how she was handling the wait.

"I wish you were here," she'd admitted.

"I know you do now. Tomorrow you'll feel differently, as soon as the two of you get used to each other again."

"If that happens," Justine had interrupted.

"Of course it will," Carter had assured her. "Within an hour, I guarantee, it'll be just like before."

"Before my accident?"

"Yes," he admitted. "That's what I meant. The accident changed many things, Justine, but they'll all fall back into place. Wait and see."

Justine had remained unsure. The nerves hadn't abated through the evening and the next morning when she'd pondered an inordinate amount of time over what to wear. She'd felt like the unsure Clara Johnson on the edge of stardom, as nervous about greeting Logan as she'd once been about greeting her fans. After weeks of indecision, everything was turning around for Justine. She'd begun to realize what was really important, and she was even more frightened than before.

Finally, after an uneasy morning that consisted of taking two long walks and flipping through a dozen or more magazines without seeing the pictures much less reading the words, Justine had returned to her high-ceilinged room on the second floor and pulled a dress out of the closet. Somehow she'd known all along that she'd wear the bright yellow sundress she'd bought on their St. Cat's shopping spree. It was all cotton, cool and simply cut. She'd worn it that night she first sang for him. She wondered if he'd remember.

From a distance, Justine was confident that she looked the same, but when she got close to the mirror she realized how much had changed since that evening only a few months before. The puffiness around her eyes and mouth had gone down, but she didn't have the same sculptured look that had once been her trademark. The scars still showed. The most recent surgery hadn't erased the last vestiges of her accident. Even the indentation below her cheek was still noticeable.

"Time," the surgeon had assured her, time and one more operation would make her as good as new. Meanwhile, she'd avoid getting close. Except that Logan was coming, and she wouldn't be able to keep her distance from him.

She'd put on very light makeup, not attempting to hide the scar, but when she got out to the veranda to wait for the Jeep to come up the drive with Steve and Angelique and Logan, Justine suddenly panicked. Turning quickly, she ran down the hall, up the stairs to her room and grabbed the straw hat and sunglasses that had become her security blanket.

Those accoutrements firmly in place, she returned to the porch to greet Logan.

Half an hour later Logan had unpacked, taken a shower and changed. Their meeting had been stilted and uncomfortable, and he'd been glad to get away to his room long enough to gather his thoughts.

Seeing her had been more jolting than he'd expected. Standing on the porch in the yellow dress he remembered so well from the early free and wonderful time together, she'd looked like a vision of everything he'd ever desired. Even in the hat and sunglasses, she was beautiful, but he'd removed both of them as soon as he was beside her on the steps. Then the look of her, the beauty and glow that he remembered yet never could quite remember perfectly had jolted him.

It had also rendered him speechless. In that awkward moment she'd stepped away, calling out to the houseboy to take the luggage up to Logan's room and suggesting that if he liked he could unpack and take a shower. Logan had agreed simply from lack of an alternate plan.

Approaching the porch again, he was glad to see that she'd left the hat and glasses on a chair beside the front door. He'd put them there when he'd whisked them off to see her better.

Now she was sitting on the porch swing, sipping a cool drink, and he wondered if she felt as cool as she looked, as calm and collected. Logan certainly didn't. He'd never felt less confident, less in charge of the situation, and he didn't know what to expect. She'd wanted him to come to St. Cat's, or she wouldn't have asked Carter to invite him. But he still didn't know why. The next move was Justine's.

She didn't seem ready to take it, but he couldn't know that what was keeping her so coolly ensconced on the swing sipping at a big glass of iced tea was a case of nerves as bad or worse than his. The houseboy's appearance at the big front door gave her a chance to speak to Logan in someone else's presence and thereby keep the tone of her voice casual. She smiled at the servant and then asked Logan without actually looking at him if he'd like a glass of iced tea.

He shook his head.

"Something else?" she tried. "A soft drink or maybe a beer?"

"No, thank you."

The houseboy left and took what modicum of calm that had existed with him, and the nerves took over. Finally Logan could stand it no longer. When he spoke he voiced not just his thoughts but hers, too. "I don't think I can stay here on this porch another minute,

Justine. Let's take a walk, or something, so I can work off this nervous energy."

Wordlessly Justine put down her drink and got up to join him but not before she reached for her straw hat and sunglasses. He thought of taking her hand and then changed his mind, instead touching her elbow gently and formally as she walked down the porch steps beside him.

The dark, nearly black ground beneath their sandaled feet was wide and smooth. The path wound through formal gardens where carefully tended orchids and obelisco bloomed radiantly. They were planted according to color, perfect groups blending one into another, purple to red to orange to yellow. Emerging from the gardens, the path narrowed, and they came upon a wilder sort of beauty. Unorganized, it assaulted Logan's eye with its cacophony of color and took his breath away. The unplanned beauty of nature had gone rampant in the deep woods. From the wildness an orchid sprouted that was unlike any he'd seen, bright violet with a defiant yellow throat.

Logan reached over and picked it and then tentatively held it out to Justine. She smiled a smile that he thought was more radiantly beautiful than the orchid and put the flower in her hair just above her ear. Then she smiled again. More than anything, he wanted to kiss her at that moment. The glossy shine of her lips captivated him and filled him with longing. He could almost taste their sweetness. It brought back the aching memory of desire.

"I'm so sorry, Logan," she said softly, and for a moment he was too deeply into his fantasy about her to understand the meaning of her words. He paused beside her, his lips mentally tasting hers and almost leaned forward into a kiss before he realized that she was talking about the last time they'd been together, the day that began with their argument over the milk shake. She was apologizing for her part in it.

"I'm sorry, too," he said as they turned together and began to walk on along the path. He reached for her hand, and she didn't resist his touch.

"You've gained a little weight," he said. "Must have kept up with the date shakes."

She smiled. "Yes, I did, although I certainly never had another one of those concoctions the nurse thought up. I've gained five pounds," she added proudly.

"Looks good on you," he said, unable to resist looking her up and down a little wickedly. "I've missed you, Justine."

The path narrowed again as they started the uphill climb, crowding them closer together and giving Logan an excuse to release her hand and put his arm snugly around her.

"I've missed you, too," she admitted. "I want to explain that remark I made about your pitying me."

He waited, aware that at last she was going to talk, and somehow knowing it would be different from the last time.

"You were right, Logan. I only said that because I pitied myself. Now I think I've gotten over the pity. Carter tells me I'm beginning to get back to normal. Whatever normal is," she added with a laugh.

"I never pitied you, Justine, but I share some of the blame for what happened between us. I didn't know how to act, so I hovered around you. And as you reminded me, I patronized you." He shook his head. "I don't know how you put up with it as long as you did."

In the distance came the sound of rushing water, a roar that made Logan stop just below the crest of the hill. "What's that? Sounds like a rapids."

"Even better," she said, delighted to be able to surprise him. "Wait until you see." She hurried ahead with a quick step, and Logan followed.

They reached the top of the hill, and there below them was a huge blue pond. It was so deep that the blue reflected from the small square of sky visible through the hordes of surrounding trees was almost purple. At one end of the pond a waterfall roared as it dropped its tons of water from twenty feet above.

"Good Lord," Logan said, "I had no idea."

"I'm so glad that I can surprise you with something on St. Cat's," she said, holding on to his hand. "I've explored the whole island, and this is my favorite spot."

"I can see why," he answered.

"I like to think of it as my own special place. Carter comes here with me sometimes, but otherwise, it's very private, secluded. I did a lot of thinking here," she told him.

"Did you find any answers?" His hand brushed across the soft flesh of her bare shoulder.

"Yes," she said. "I believe I did. Finally. It's taken me a long time."

He didn't ask her about the answers. He knew that she'd tell him in time, and he knew from the way she looked at him that he'd been in her thoughts and was in them still.

"Let me show you the waterfall from up close," she said. With her hand still in his, Justine walked down the hill beside him. They circled the pond toward the waterfall. "If we run, we can get under the falls without getting soaked," she suggested.

"Let's go," he said, grabbing her hand. He rushed with her across the smooth rocks at the edge of the pond, and then they ducked around, keeping close to the bank until they were in the cavelike space behind the falls.

"Well, not completely soaked, anyway," Logan said with a laugh as he shook the water out of his hair.

"But worth it," Justine reminded him.

They stood back in the shadows of the steep bank as the waterfall cascaded a few feet in front of them, sending sparkling sprays upward from the pond, catching in the sun and creating a rainbow, an exotic show of dancing light and water.

"Definitely worth it." Logan put one arm around Justine's shoulder and turned her toward him. "I'm glad to be here with you," he said. Moving away from the water, he sat down beside her on a mossy rock. "Tell me about the answers you found."

Here under the falls he felt a certain ease with her at last. Her smile showed that at least she shared the peacefulness of the place. "Tell me," he said again.

"I decided that I've been a fool."

"No," he said, touching her face lightly.

"Oh, yes. I thought of my accident as a terrible trick fate played on me. It's not that at all. After two months I realize the good that came with all the pain."

Logan felt himself wince at the memory of her pain.

"It's all right," she said. "It's over. My accident, the forced retirement, served a purpose after all. It's as if fate wasn't playing games but was telling me, 'Enough, Justine; it's time for a real life, a life with

Logan.' I was wrong," she told him softly, "when I said I shouldn't marry you."

Logan reached up and took off her straw hat. "You can put that on when we go back. As for these, I think it's time to get rid of them for good," he said, removing her sunglasses and tossing them out into the tumbling water.

"Logan."

He silenced her lips with a kiss. It was their first real kiss in two months, tender and inquisitive. Trembling lips met trembling lips as if for the first time as they both became infused with recognition and desire.

"Justine." Logan took her face in his hands and looked down at her. "I'm so glad to have you back," he whispered just before he kissed her again.

This time Justine let herself melt into the kiss and into Logan's arms, wonderfully loved and wanted again. For so long she'd needed to feel his strong arms around her. Now they were together again at last, and she was safe.

"I'll count to ten," Logan said teasingly against her ear, "and then let's get out of here fast."

Hugging and kissing, damp from the spray of the falls, they made their way back to Savoy's Revenge, up the wide staircase and down the hall to Justine's room, where they stood, hair wet and skin glistening, clothes hanging limply. It was sweet and tender their reunion, and it was so filled with love that they both trembled beneath the force of it.

For a long moment they stood at the foot of the four-poster bed looking, smiling, in memory and anticipation. Then Logan reached out and unbuttoned her sundress, peeling it from her shoulders so he could kiss the bare skin. He used his tongue to taste the salty sweetness of her as he pulled the damp sundress down to her waist. Deepening the kiss, his mouth covered hers.

Logan's polo shirt stuck wetly to his skin, but Justine managed to slip her hands beneath it to feel the body that she'd been aching to touch for more than two months. She shivered with desire as she held him at last, pressing him close, overcome by the need for him that had never left her after all that time.

The sweetness of their newly discovered love remained, but it was no longer tentative. Now it was as greedy, as demanding as the kiss that they gave themselves to. Continuing that kiss, they somehow managed to slip off their clothes and leave them in a pile at the foot of the bed.

Justine shivered again, partly from the chill of the air on her damp, naked skin, mostly from the look in Logan's eyes and the catch in his voice.

"Justine," he said, reaching out to take her hand, "I feel like I'm seeing you for the first time." He let his hand trail up her arm to her shoulder. "Touching you for the first time." He leaned over until his lips found hers again. "Kissing you for..." He never finished the thought because the kiss deepened as their bare bodies came together gently and then powerfully, her breasts crushed against the dark hair of his chest, his hard arousal against her feathery mound, skin to skin, flesh holding and kneading flesh, mouths claiming mouths.

Time rushed backward and they were the lovers they'd been that first day long ago on the beach of St. Cat's. Logan bent over and took Justine in his arms and carried her around the bed to put her on the cool sheets. Overhead the fan droned lazily; through the windows the sun washed them with its white glow. "I'm so glad it's daylight so I can see you while I make love to you," Logan said huskily as he lay down beside her.

After so long away from the sun, Justine's skin was creamy porcelain once more. The freckles across her nose had disappeared, the evidence of sunburn had vanished. Her pale skin made her hair seem more fiery red, her eyes more deeply brown, her lips pinker than ever.

Logan shook his head in delight. "You're beautiful," he whispered.

Justine heard the words and believed them. There beneath his loving gaze with his hands so lightly caressing her, she knew that she was beautiful. When he kissed her again, she knew that she was loved as she'd never been loved before and would never be loved again. Her whole body opened to him.

His hands reached out and touched her breasts. They were soft and pliant beneath his exploring fingertips, but her nipples were taut when he brushed them with his palm. Logan used his tongue to invade her mouth as his fingers teased. He could feel the heat of her passion on the surface of her skin. It seemed to be pouring from her into his waiting hands. It burned his palms and surged through his body. He had to force himself to hold back and find the gentleness that he'd meant to bring to this renewed love and need for her.

He found it in her eyes that looked at him, shining with love and trust as much as with need and desire. He smiled down at her and with caring hands parted her legs and slipped inside her sweet moistness, her waiting warmth. All the time that had passed since they'd last made love was compressed in this one moment, and all the love she'd ever known was here and now as she held him deeply within her, filled with his love as she was filled with him.

The gentleness of his movement within her was such that Justine felt herself transported out of reality into a dreamlike state in which there was only the barest touch of body upon body. Then she lifted her hips to meet him, and the movement made him cry out in passion. He gathered her in his arms and moved eagerly within her. She was brought back from the dream to feel every fiber of her being covered with him, filled with him, holding and kissing and smelling and tasting him. His hot flesh was slippery beneath her greedy hands. His tongue invaded her mouth that was welcoming as her body welcomed his manhood.

In one long, quivering, endless moment they reached the pinnacle of their joy together and called out in unison as the white rays of the sun bathed them in a brightness that equalled their passion. Then heavily they collapsed together, wrapped in each other's arms, breathing hard, hearts pounding.

Exhausted and spent, they still were able to laugh aloud in their joy and whisper fragments of loving sentences before falling deeply asleep, wrapped together. For both of them it was a long, delicious slumber, the most complete and untroubled in all the weeks since they'd been apart, alone and lonely yet not allowing themselves to admit that loneliness.

Justine admitted it later when they awoke together, stretched and snuggled in each other's arms. "I missed you so. All those hours and days of thinking about myself, I was really thinking of you, imagining you, fantasizing you.''

"I know, my love," he answered, smoothing back the curly hair from her forehead. "I've been living in that same fantasy and wondering if it would ever be real again. Thank God it *is* real now." He kissed her lazily.

But the passion that had brought them from their race through the woods to Justine's bed had not abated after their lovemaking and the long sleep that followed. It had reawakened in them all the long-lost need for each other, the excitement, the way they fit together, belonged together, the mutual admiration that was a part of the attraction. All those things made up their love and turned it into hot desire. A lazy kiss became a probing kiss, hands wandered, lips tasted, eyes smiled and then sparkled as their desire ignited again, more brightly even than before. It blotted out everything—time, place, even St. Cat's itself. Their love was all.

Two hours later they sat sedately across from each other at the formal dining room table. Carter's butler, immaculately garbed, hovered nearby to serve them. The candles blazed elegantly in silver holders. The centerpiece, more extravagant than usual, once more blocked the view across the table, and Logan quickly remedied that by moving it aside so he could look into her eyes.

Their conversation while the butler remained in the room concerned Logan's trip from New York, the weather he left behind, the weather he found here, and touched playfully on Steve and Angelique.

"They're getting married this summer, Steve tells me."

"Yes," Justine answered. "Carter will be sorry to lose Angelique, and I'm sure Monsieur Moreau will be, too."

Logan laughed. "Moreau might actually have to do a little work on his own now that she's moving out."

"Oh, I imagine he'll find a way to avoid that," Justine answered.

The butler had taken away their soup and gone into the kitchen for the next course. Logan looked after him and said, "You were a tiger today after you woke up."

"Ssh," Justine sounded as the door swung open again and the butler returned with their main course, leaving Logan quiet but not without a twinkle in his eye.

They got through dinner that way with Logan's outrageous remarks fitted between courses and Justine's blushes undiminished from soup through dessert. As she finished her last sip of coffee, Justine suggested they go out to the veranda, heard with relief Logan's agreement and then held her breath until they were out of earshot of the butler.

"Did I embarrass you?" Logan asked.

Justine tried to poke him in the ribs and missed as he led the way to the veranda and the slatted green porch swing. "I've always wanted one of these," Logan said. "They're so..."

"Old-fashioned," Justine finished.

"Exactly. Everything in this wonderful house is straight out of a 1940s movie."

"I know." Justine sat down beside him and leaned her head against his shoulder as Logan pushed with his feet until the swing began to creak gently along. "Isn't it romantic, the house?"

Logan smiled. "Especially with you in it. Now, to continue what we were talking about under your waterfall today." He smiled again, sexily, and she returned the smile, remembering how their conversation had been interrupted. "You were saying that you wanted to marry me."

"Logan, that makes me sound so blatant." Justine, amused, didn't notice the serious expression on Logan's face. "My actual words were, 'I was wrong when I said I shouldn't marry you.'"

"I think we need to talk about that, Justine."

She realized his seriousness then and felt herself stiffen against him.

"I love you," he said. "You know that. This afternoon only reinforced the way I've felt all along, but I don't think..." He seemed to stumble over the words. "I don't want to marry you now."

Justine tried not to react, but she knew that her body language was giving her away.

It was. "Now, listen to me, Justine," Logan said in a reassuring voice. "I don't want to marry you when you have no other options. I've had time to think, too, and I'll be damned if I'll be guilty of rescuing you or patronizing you. You'd never forgive me for that."

Justine still wasn't sure what he was saying, where the conversation was going. She tried to clear her head of doubts and listen to his words.

"Justine, I'm telling you that I want to marry you, but not until you're back on top and you can say, 'I still want Logan.'"

Justine's feet barely reached the floor, but she managed to stop the movement of the swing and look up at him. "Until I'm back on top?" The look on her face was disbelieving. "Logan, I'm not going to perform again. I can't do that. I . . ."

"Yes, you can. I know it. So does Adele. We all know you can do it, Justine."

"No," she said shakily. "I told you, Logan, I want to be your wife. I want to marry you and be Mrs. Logan Addison. That's all I want."

He looked down at her, his eyes narrowing. "No, it's not, Justine."

"I know what I want," she defended.

"You know what's safe. Right now you don't know what's possible. I'm going to see that you have a chance to regain the career you once said you could never give up."

"That was before. We're talking about now."

"You're still Justine."

Justine turned her head away, and for the first time since they'd been together that day, she was aware of the surgery, remembering the scar.

Logan took her face in both of his hands and turned it back toward him. "Listen, you little idiot, you're better than ever, but I would love you no matter how you looked. All I want is for you to understand that and love me as unequivocally. I want you to say, 'I have fame, and I have Logan.' Then I want you to choose. Choose one, choose both, but choose. I can handle your fame if you decide you want to share it with me. If not, well, that's a chance I have to take. I might lose you, but it's the only way. You've got to go back on stage first before you make any other decisions."

Justine hadn't expected this. "I've thought it all out, Logan," she said. "That's why I needed the time.

I've made my decision. I can't go back on the stage. I can't ever go back." She knew that she was almost crying, but there was nothing she could do about it. "To sing again, to perform . . . I can't."

"You have to. Don't you see that there's no other way for us? When I met you, you were at the top. You were Justine. When I marry you I still want you to have that choice. It's just a choice, my love, but you have to go back to the top so you can make it honestly."

"How can I?" She whispered the question, her voice filled with hopelessness. "How can I? Do you know what you're asking?"

"I'm asking no more than you're capable of delivering."

Justine shook her head as her feet brushed the floor, starting the movement of the swing again. "I don't know."

"Say that you'll try," he urged.

She looked up at him and suddenly understood that with Logan beside her, she could do it or at least she could try.

"And Justine." He tightened his arm around her shoulder. "I want you to pick up exactly where you left. I want you to sing again at La Quinta."

Everything was different the night at Cabaret La Quinta when Justine came back. The electricity in the air as the audience waited for her to appear was expectant but hushed, mixed with tension. The excitement was of a sort that Logan had never felt anywhere before. It seemed as if the whole room had taken a collective breath, and the tension was palpable.

Logan had booked a small table beside the stage where Carter joined him. There was none of the joviality that had existed at Justine's last opening, for this wasn't an opening at all. It was a one-night performance slipped in between two other bookings, a test that Justine was giving herself to see if she could do it.

Until that afternoon, no one even knew she was appearing. The press hadn't been alerted. Frank and Diane weren't there, and neither was Adele. Justine had asked them not to come because she didn't want to turn this one night into a big event. She wanted it to be just another show. But it would never be anything less than what it was, Justine Hart's comeback.

Although no press releases had been sent out, two reporters had apparently gotten wind of the story as they always seemed to, Logan thought when he spied their faces in the audience. "The press is here," he told Carter.

"Good," came the reply. Carter calmly lit a slim black cigar. "She'll be sensational, and they'll know about it, not just in this room but everywhere. That's the way it should be."

Backstage, Justine sat alone in the dressing room. Unable to stand the confusion, the hovering and pampering, she'd sent everyone away. She was dressed and ready and didn't need them, and she thought she wanted to be alone. As soon as the door closed and left her there in the empty little room, Justine realized that she'd made a mistake. She needed people around her in these last minutes, but she was determined not to make a fool of herself by bringing them back.

When her first call came, Justine almost got up and walked away, out of the dressing room, down the hall and into the night. She almost gave in to the nerves that had taken hold of her so completely. But she didn't walk away, even though the words to her opening number had gone out of her head completely. Somehow she got into position as the band began the overture. She got that far, she did that much, for Logan. But she couldn't take the next step.

With the sound of the band building came the memory of last time, the light crashing toward her, the pain, the weeks of uncertainty that had followed the decision not to return to the stage. Now she could hear the applause. It began to grow louder.

It had all seemed so simple, so easy, her settled life with Logan. Then before she even knew what was happening, he'd arranged this return to La Quinta. That had been wrong of him. She'd never be able to live up to the expectations of the people waiting in the audience. She didn't look like Justine anymore. She wasn't Justine anymore, and she didn't want to be. She didn't want to take the chance.

The applause grew louder, and Justine closed her eyes and shook her head. She couldn't go on.

The moment of denial seemed to last forever and then, somehow, Justine managed to step onto the stage. The lights caught her eyes and she was blinded. Forgetting her promise to herself not to look up, she focused on *that* place, *that* light. As she stared and remembered, the music screamed in her ears, strange and unfamiliar. She could never sing along with it; she still couldn't remember the first line, the first word. Why had she let Logan force her into this? Why? Blind panic enveloped her.

Watching from his table nearby, Logan felt as if a giant hand had constricted around his throat. He was

scared to death for her, and there wasn't a damn thing
he could do but sit there and hope he hadn't made a
tragic mistake. The initial applause faded, the introduction began and still Justine stood there, looking
small and brave and very much alone. Tears stung
Logan's eyes. He wanted to leave his table, rush to her
and sweep her from the stage. Feverishly, he prayed
that she would make it, that his decision had been the
right one.

When Justine missed her first cue, the band leader
segued once more into the introduction, a frown
creasing his brow, for Justine remained immobile as a
statue. The audience's silence hung like an eerie pall
over the room. It was almost palpable, as if waiting for
disaster to happen.

The band held the last notes an extra measure until
Justine, like a puppet pulled by unseen hands, began
to move and then to sing, on beat but shaky, unsure.

I see the writing on the wall...

Logan heard the quivering strains and pushed himself to his feet. Rehearsal had been one thing, but to
bring her here, to force her to repeat an episode that
could only bring back horrible memories was more
cruel than kind. The blood was pounding in Logan's
head so loudly he couldn't hear the music or Justine's
voice. He had but one thought, to go to her and hold
her and make everything all right.

Something stopped him. It was Carter's hand on his
arm, pulling him back into the chair. "It's all right,
Logan. Just listen to her. Justine is back!"

On the stage, Justine sang for Logan, and for him
alone just as she'd sung for him at St. Cat's, and he

heard her, heard the true, clear and incomparable voice of Justine. He knew that Carter was right. She was back, singing their song unending.

> My applause
> Is my tomorrow
> With you.

She held the last note clearly, sublimely, into infinity it seemed. That note sang in Logan's head and in his heart. As the audience surged to its feet, he let his tears fall.

Two hours later the applause had finally died down and faded away. She'd done it. Justine stood in the hallway behind the stage surrounded by a blur of voices and faces. Through the haze she saw Logan leaning against the doorway of her dressing room, slightly removed from the crowd, his hands in his pockets, a half smile on his face.

Before she could even smile back, the crowd enveloped Justine. She recognized a few of the people closest to her and tried to acknowledge their praise, still straining to keep Logan in her view. Then she heard Carter's voice.

"You were just wonderful, as I expected, my dear." He sneaked a quick kiss on Justine's cheek. "Now, shall I get rid of this crowd?"

He'd seen that Justine couldn't keep her gaze away from the door, where Logan still waited, silently. "Yes," she whispered. "If you would just tell everyone to give me a few minutes." With that she crossed to where Logan stood, took his arm and pulled him into her dressing room.

Grinning, he closed the door behind them and wrapped her in his arms. "Pretty soon they'll be trying to break down the door," he reminded her between kisses.

"Let them," she murmured. "I need this time to thank you, Logan, for giving me Justine."

"You don't owe me any thanks, my darling," he answered. "You were always sensational, and you still are—it's as simple as that."

He turned her toward her mirror, and she stood for a moment looking at herself reflected there. She saw in her face the flush of success. "It feels good," she said slowly. "Performing, knowing the audience loves me. I need that, Logan," she added, turning to him.

"I know you do." As he spoke his heart began to ache. He'd told her to come back, forced her back, and all the while somewhere inside there'd been the hope that after her triumph, she would be able to give it all up. That hadn't happened, and he really hadn't expected it to. She'd come back and she was back to stay. He had to say the words before she said them. "I know you can't give it up."

She turned away from the mirror. Standing tall, she lifted her chin and held her head high. "There's nothing I can't do. If you still want to marry me, I can leave all this." Speaking the words aloud, she knew they were true and they gave her strength.

Logan stepped away, his heart pounding, heady with excitement. He could have her all to himself, he could take her away from this, but if he did, he knew she'd be leaving part of herself behind. "No," he said, turning toward her. "I want to marry you, but I don't want you to give this up."

Justine uttered a little sigh and rushed to him. "I know that," she said, putting her arms around his neck. "And I love you for it." She kissed him, again and again. "Oh, I do love you. You will marry me, won't you, Logan?"

Logan laughed. "Just try to stop me," he said, returning all of her kisses before taking her face in his hands and looking into her eyes in earnest.

Justine smiled up at him. "I've found that real world we've been looking for, Logan. It's inside of us wherever we are, just as long as we're together."

"And we're *always* going to be together." He kissed her again and wrapped her in his arms, trying to ignore the insistent noise from outside the door. "Your groupies are just going to have to get used to waiting when I'm around," he said. "They can go to your concerts if they want to, and they can get your autograph." He kissed her again. "You can even sing your songs for them—on the stage. All the rest of the time, your song will be for me alone."

COMING NEXT MONTH

CRISTEN'S CHOICE—Ginna Gray
Finding a blatantly virile, nearly naked man in her bathroom gave Cristen
the shock of her life. But Ryan O'Malley's surprises didn't stop there,
and his teasing sensual tactics left her limp with longing—and
perpetually perplexed!

PURPLE DIAMONDS—Jo Ann Algermissen
When beautiful heartbreaker Halley Twain was assigned to his ward,
Dr. Mark Abraham knew she meant danger. After reopening his old
emotional wounds, would she have the healing touch to save him?

WITH THIS RING—Pat Warren
Nick flipped over kooky Kate Stevens, but she was his brother's girlfriend,
and the two men already had a score to settle. Still, Nick couldn't stop
himself from wanting her.

RENEGADE SON—Lisa Jackson
With her farm in jeopardy, Dani would do anything to save it. But when
sexy, rugged Chase McEnroe seemed determined to take it from her, she
wondered just how far she'd have to go....

A MEASURE OF LOVE—Lindsay McKenna
Jessie had come to protect wild horses, but one look at proud, defiant
rancher Rafe Kincaid was enough to warn her—it was her heart that was
in danger.

HIGH SOCIETY—Lynda Trent
Their families had feuded for years, but mechanic Mike Barlow and
socialite Sheila Danforth felt nothing but attraction. Could the heat of
their kisses ever melt society's icy disdain?

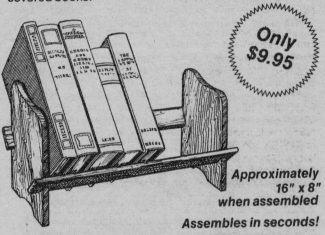

Take 4 Silhouette Romance novels
FREE

Then preview 6 brand-new Silhouette Romance® novels—delivered to your door as soon as they are published—for 15 days without obligation. When you decide to keep them, pay just $1.95 each, *with no shipping, handling or other charges of any kind!*

Each month, you'll meet lively young heroines and share in their thrilling escapades, trials and triumphs... virile men you'll find as attractive and irresistible as the heroines do... and colorful supporting characters you'll feel you've always known.

Start with 4 Silhouette Romance novels absolutely FREE. They're yours to keep without obligation, and you can cancel at any time.

As an added bonus, you'll also get the Silhouette Books Newsletter FREE with every shipment. Every issue is filled with news on upcoming books, interviews with your favorite authors, even their favorite recipes.

Simply fill out and return the coupon today!
This offer is not available in Canada.

Silhouette Books, 120 Brighton Rd., P.O. Box 5084, Clifton, NJ 07015-5084

Clip and mail to: Silhouette Books,
120 Brighton Road, P.O. Box 5084, Clifton, NJ 07015-5084

YES. Please send me 4 Silhouette Romance novels FREE. Unless you hear from me after I receive them, send me six new Silhouette Romance novels to preview each month as soon as they are published. I understand you will bill me just $1.95 each (a total of $11.70) with no shipping, handling, or other charges of any kind. There is no minimum number of books that I must buy, and I can cancel at any time. The first 4 books are mine to keep.   **81RS87**

Name _____ (please print)

Address _____ Apt. #

City _____ State _____ Zip _____

Terms and prices subject to change. Not available in Canada.   **SilR-SUB-1A**
SILHOUETTE ROMANCE is a service mark and registered trademark.

FOUR UNIQUE SERIES
FOR EVERY WOMAN YOU ARE . . .

Silhouette Romance

Heartwarming romances that will make you
laugh and cry as they bring you all the wonder
and magic of falling in love.

6 titles per month

Silhouette Special Edition

Expanded romances written with emotion and
heightened romantic tension to ensure
powerful stories. A rare blend of passion and
dramatic realism.

6 titles per month

Silhouette Desire

Believable, sensuous, compelling—and
above all, romantic—these stories deliver
the promise of love, the guarantee
of satisfaction.

6 titles per month

Silhouette Intimate Moments

Love stories that entice; longer, more
sensuous romances filled with adventure,
suspense, glamour and melodrama.

4 titles per month

Silhouette Romances
not available in retail outlets in Canada

SIL-GEN-1A